The Summer of Guinevere

by

John V. Madormo

The Summer of Guinevere

Cover Art by *Kim Mendoza*

The Wild Rose Press, Inc.
PO Box 708
Adams Basin, NY 14410-0708
Visit us at www.thewildrosepress.com

Publishing History
First New Adult Edition, 2019
Print ISBN 978-1-5092-2522-4
Digital ISBN 978-1-5092-2523-1

Published in the United States of America

Before our conversation could continue, I heard the same sound I had heard earlier—the pickup with the muffler problem. It was coming back the other way now. I focused on the bed, hoping for a glimpse of that great-looking girl. As it approached, it slowed down a little. There were still the three boys in the back, and standing up behind the cab, there she was. My eyes were glued to her. It seemed like she was looking right at me again as they passed. Boy, she was gorgeous.

"Hey, give him a little kiss, why don't you," one of the boys yelled out. He seemed to be aiming his jab at Uncle Buddy.

I could hear them laughing as the truck continued down the road.

"What was that kid talking about?" I asked.

"Oh, don't pay any attention to them," Uncle Buddy said. "They're up to no good."

But I wanted to know more about them, especially the girl. What was her name? How old was she? Did she come by here often? Where did she live? Did she have a boyfriend?

I wanted to know everything about her.

Praise for John V. Madormo's first novel, *THE HOMEMADE STUFFING CAPER*

Bank Street College of Education (NY) Best Children's Books of 2013

The International Spy Museum's (Washington, DC) list of Recommended Books

Barnes and Noble's "Must Read" list (2012)

Family Fun Magazine's List of Recommended Books for Kids (2012)

Chicago Public Schools Battle of the Books (2013-14)

Quizlet's (national) Battle of the Books (2013-14)

Novel Quest (national) Battle of the Books (2013-14)

Des Moines (IA) Public Schools Battle of the Books (2013-14)

Dedication

To my college sweetheart and
spouse of 44 wonderful years, Celeste

For more information about this novel and the author, please visit www.summerofguinevere.com

Chapter 1

Chicago. August 1968. A summer I will never forget. The city and the nation were still reeling from a pair of assassinations. In April, Dr. Martin Luther King, Jr. had been cut down by a sniper in Memphis. In the days that followed, the City of Big Shoulders mourned, but it also burned. And in June, Senator Bobby Kennedy, while on a presidential campaign swing in California, found himself in the crosshairs of another madman's sights. For some reason these events really didn't bother me. And it bothered me they didn't. These were tragic, earth-shattering occurrences. I should have been reading the paper or watching the news—but I wasn't. What was wrong with me? Was I heartless? Was I apathetic?

I remember asking my best friend, Mickey Hannigan, if there was something odd about the fact I didn't seem to care much about world events. He told me we had seen so many murders on TV and at the movies in our lifetime we had become numb to killing. The fact these were real people who had lost their lives didn't seem to matter. "Things like this happen," Mickey would say. "We read about them all the time in history books, so why would anybody be so shocked when they take place in our lifetimes? Listen, Paulie, the world is filled with lunatics. These things were bound to happen."

It was weird, though, to think fifty or a hundred years from now, kids would be studying the same stuff in history classes we were watching on the evening news, or rather, not watching. I knew this was really important stuff. So why was I more concerned about what was happening in my own life? I didn't know. Maybe there *was* something wrong with me. I usually found myself more worried about things some people might regard as trivial—like getting my driver's license—or wondering if I'd be invited to a particular party—or if I'd ever work up the nerve to ask a girl out on a date.

Let's face it. When you're in high school, it's all about social status, not the ten o'clock news. You'd never find anyone willing to admit it, but everyone knew it was true. It was all about who your friends were, what sport you excelled in, or what kind of car you drove. I was embarrassed to say I had managed to strike out on all three fronts. If I had to describe my life to someone, I could have summed it up in one word— bleak. It wasn't fair. I didn't deserve this. A few years ago, things were different. Back in grammar school, I was one of the popular kids, or at least I thought I was. But now I was just one of the lemmings. I had allowed myself to become a follower. I simply blended in. There was nothing special about me anymore. And I hated it. When I entered high school, I had such big plans. I was going to blaze a trail. I was going to make people take notice. I was going to be, well, popular. Not on the football field or basketball court. I hadn't been blessed with those talents. Instead I planned to wow them academically and politically and socially. I saw myself as valedictorian and class president and king of the homecoming court. In the yearbook, it would say I had been voted as "Most likely to succeed—at everything." I had it all planned out.

So there I was, about to enter my junior year, with nothing to show for myself but a bunch of mediocre grades and a handful of "acquaintances." I really couldn't call any of them friends. My only real friend was Mickey Hannigan. The Mick and I were inseparable. We had attended grammar school together, and now we were locker partners in high school—Anton J. Cermak College Prep. The Mick and I were a team. We did everything together. I didn't know what I'd do after graduation. He and I were headed in different directions. Mick had already picked out a dozen colleges. I, on the other hand, wasn't really sure if I'd ever cut it in college. I sure didn't want to pump gas or work in some factory after high school, but I was afraid it would be even worse if I started out at some college and then flunked out. It would be easier to say I wasn't going because I didn't want to. As painful as it was to say, Mick was not only my best friend, he was my only real friend. There—I said it. I had a hard time fitting in. It wasn't as if I was some kind of a freak. I was average-looking if you didn't count my nose. I had what people called a Roman nose. It was *roamin'* all over my face. My mom used to tell me it made me look distinguished. Yeah, right. What else would a mother tell you?

I was what you might call an underachiever. My parents knew it. My teachers knew it. I knew it. I wasn't a dumb kid, mind you. I just didn't *apply* myself. That was how my dad described it. He called it *an inability to take responsibility for my own education.*

What was he bitching about? He didn't have to pay for it. I wasn't in one of those preppy, private schools. I wished everyone would just leave me alone. So you can see why I wasn't really looking forward to returning to school in September and claiming my position as an upperclassman. It meant nothing to me. It just meant pretty much more of the same—the same old crap. I was in a rut—a permanent rut. With no escape on the horizon.

As was usually the case in the dog days of summer, the Mick and I were holed up in my room. Mick had eaten dinner with us, and we were chowing down a pair of ice cream sandwiches.

"What are you afraid of?" Mickey said. "They don't bite, for Pete's sake."

"I'm not afraid," I said defensively. But I was. And he could tell. It was that sixth sense a best friend has.

"I didn't want to be the one to say this, but somebody has to," he said as he cleared his throat.

Oh, great. Now what?

"You're sixteen years old and you haven't gone out on a date yet?" He popped the last piece of ice cream sandwich into his mouth and tossed the wrapper into the wastebasket. Then he stood there with this smug look and folded his arms. "People'll think there's something wrong with you."

"Oh, and you're such a ladykiller, is that it?" I fired back.

No one had to remind me I was no Don Juan. I was outgoing—well, sort of. It was almost easier for me to talk to adults than kids my own age. I guess it was because we spent every Sunday afternoon at my grandmother's house surrounded by countless aunts and

4

uncles. That was my mom's mom, by the way. I had never actually met my dad's parents. They weren't dead or anything. But I'd never seen them. It was a long story. More on that later. I resumed my verbal tussle with Mickey.

"Well, I'm a little more experienced than you are," he said.

"*Little* is right." To be precise, Mickey had gone on two dates in his entire life. One you really couldn't count. It was with his cousin. And the other was a blind date fix-up with the daughter of a lady in his mom's book club. He took her to Kiddieland, a local amusement park. The night started out all right, but the ending was nothing short of a disaster. Following a spin on the Tilt-a-Whirl, the Mick proceeded to throw up. Now that was what I call impressing your date. And if that wasn't bad enough, did I happen to mention he hurled *on* his date? Needless to say, they never hooked up again. So, based on his mediocre track record with the fair sex, where was he getting off giving me grief about girls?

"I plan to ask someone out this year," I said. "You can book it."

"This year? What's that supposed to mean?"

"I can't give you an exact date."

Mickey shook his head. "This is a waste of time."

I plopped down on my bed and curled up into a fetal position for effect. "Why is this so important to you anyway?"

Mickey slid over on the tile floor, sat down on the edge of the bed, and punched me in the shoulder.

"Hey, what was that for?" I said as I rubbed the affected area.

"Listen, Paulie, I've decided to make you my personal project this year. I'll get you a date if it kills me. And if you're lucky, I might get you multiple dates. Maybe even a girlfriend."

I sat up. "You? You're going to get me a girlfriend?" I laughed. "I might have more faith in your abilities as a matchmaker if you had your own girlfriend. But that's about as unlikely as me having one."

Mickey made a face. I think he was a little hurt.

"Listen, Mick, I appreciate your interest in my love life, but this is something I have to do on my own. You don't have to worry about me. I've got a plan. In a few weeks, I'll be putting it into action. And before you know it, there's gonna be *babes galore*."

The Mick scratched his head and smiled. "Well, you certainly have my attention. I want to hear more about this plan of yours. It sounds interesting."

I popped up, walked to the window, and stared down at my dad in the backyard pulling weeds from around the flowers.

"I haven't completely fleshed it out. It's got a lot of angles to it. You'll just have to wait."

"A lot of angles?" Mickey shook his head. "No offense, but you're full of it."

I sighed. "You'll see."

Mickey walked over, grabbed me by the shoulders, and spun me around. "Spill it, partner. I want the name of your first conquest. Who is she? Give me that, and I won't ask you for any more details."

I knew the only way to shut him up was to give him what he wanted. The problem was I didn't have a name because there was no plan. I just figured if I told him that, I'd be able to buy myself a little time.

"I knew it," he said. "You got nothing."

And then before I knew what had happened, I had blurted out a name. "Violet."

The Mick looked confused. "Violet who?"

"I don't know her last name."

A smile suddenly appeared on Mickey's face. "The girl on our bus? The blonde with the heavy eye make-up?"

I nodded.

"Paulie, she doesn't even go to our school. She goes to Ridgeway. She's way out of your league, pal. Girls like that'll eat you alive."

Every morning when school was in session, I'd meet the Mick at the bus stop on Belmont. We didn't ride the big yellow school buses. It wasn't like that. We were world travelers. We rode the CTA—the Chicago Transit Authority. When the green-and-yellow bus pulled up, we'd hop on, flash our student IDs, and drop forty cents into the plastic box next to the driver, who would usually sneer at us. Then we'd scoot to the rear of the bus. No self-respecting teenage male would be caught dead in the front seats. Those were reserved for old ladies with shopping bags who were going who knows where. And forget the middle seats. Those were for working class stiffs who carried brown or silver lunch boxes. Although there was no signage to support it, the back of the bus was reserved for kids.

That was where I was sitting when I first saw Violet. I only knew her name because I heard someone call out to her once. Violet got on the bus a couple of stops after us, and she got off at Narragansett Avenue, where all the Ridgeway kids exited. I used to love watching her walk down the middle aisle. She had this long blonde hair parted down the middle and a little poofed up in the back. She wore short skirts and black stockings, and she was always chewing gum. This girl was a goddess. My only complaint was her eye makeup. She put it on really thick. You couldn't help but be drawn to her eyes. They just jumped off her face. I used to fantasize about going out with her and telling her she was such a natural beauty she didn't need to wear makeup, especially the black eye liner and shadow. But I knew a conversation like that would never take place because in order to go on a date with a girl, you actually had to talk to a girl.

I was always so jealous of the guys who could just walk up to girls at a sock-hop and ask them to dance. Can you believe it? There were actually guys out there who could approach a complete stranger and start talking to her. As badly as I wanted to, I could never see myself doing that. The irony was I would attend most of the sock-hops but never dance. I would try to look cool. I used to find someone from one of my classes and just babble endlessly about a lot of nothing until the other fellow got bored and walked away. Occasionally a guy I knew would walk by, poke me on the shoulder, point to a girl, and suggest I ask her to dance. Yeah, like that was ever going to happen. I always hated that because I knew I'd never build up the nerve to act on the suggestion, but I didn't want to look like some pantywaist too afraid to talk to a girl. After a handful of painful experiences, I figured out a way to handle the problem. I came up with a dozen or so makeshift excuses and stashed them in my arsenal. Now whenever someone pressured me to take action, I would rattle off a canned line to save face. "That song is too fast." "That song is too slow." "Oh, I know her and she's a real pain in the ass." "She's with a group of friends. You can't ask just one of them. The others would feel bad." "Are you kidding? She's a beast." And on and on.

"What makes you think you'd have a chance in hell of asking out Violet?" Mickey said. "If you got within ten feet of her, that Ridgeway posse of hers would cut you off at the knees."

"I guess you'll just have to wait and see the magic for yourself," I said smugly.

We were distracted by a knock on the bedroom door.

"Come in."

My mom poked her head in. "I don't want to break things up, boys, but it's getting late. Paulie, you should really be packing for the trip." She smiled and ducked out.

"Trip?" Mickey said. "What trip?"

"It's a long story, Mick. I have to go with my dad back to a little town where he grew up."

"Where at?"

"Some dinky rat-infested town in Pennsylvania."

"Pennsylvania? How long will you be gone?"

"A week. Maybe two. I don't know."

Mickey put his hands on his hips. "And when were you gonna tell me? You know, best friends don't keep secrets from each other."

"Well, it's not really a secret. I just forgot to tell you."

Mickey shook his head disgustedly. "Why are you goin' anyhow?"

"My dad's mother—my grandmother, I guess—is dying."

Mickey cocked his head to one side. "You *guess* she's your grandmother? What's that supposed to mean? Either she is or she isn't."

"She *is*. It's just that I've never met her. And to top it off, my dad hasn't seen her in more than twenty years."

The Mick fell back onto the bed. "Whoa!" He shook his head.

I shrugged. "It's a long story."

"So, what am I supposed to do for the next two weeks?" he said.

"I don't know what to tell you. I can't do anything about it. My dad said I have to go, so I have to go. You can't win an argument with him."

Mickey glanced at the clock radio on the dresser. "Oh, man, I gotta get going." He jumped up. "Call me as soon as you're back in town. You got it?"

I nodded and walked him downstairs and into the living room, where my mom was paging through the TV guide.

"Thanks again for dinner, Mrs. Passero. It was really good. What was that meat thing again—the one tied up with a string?"

"It's called *braciole*," my mom said. "It's flank steak with a filling of bread crumbs, garlic, onion, parsley, Parmesan..." She stopped in mid-sentence. "You're not interested in all that. But thanks for the compliment."

"Maybe you could teach my mom how to make it."

"If she's interested, I'd be more than happy to give her the recipe."

It was weird hearing someone thanking my mom for a meal we saw at least once a week. Sometimes I would forget what a great cook she was. I guess we just took it for granted. My mom cooked up a dinner from scratch every night whether she wanted to or not. My dad was old school. He had no interest in restaurant food. And why would you when you had a wife who could outcook the best restaurants in town? Sometimes I thought about sabotaging the stove just so we could get some fast food. If I wanted a burger and fries, I'd have to pay for it myself.

I waved goodbye to Mickey and retreated to the solitude of my room. I thought more about the proposition of asking out Violet. It was an insane idea. Why had I even suggested it? Something like that would never happen. And not because I was afraid to talk to her, which of course I was, but because she just wasn't my type. I wasn't into the ratted hair and heavy makeup. I was more into natural beauty. You know, the more athletic, wholesome types. The ones with hair that flies around on a windy day. Violet and her friends used way too much hair spray. Their hair never moved, not even in a monsoon. It was like they were wearing helmets.

So why did I throw out Violet's name if I had no intention of ever speaking to her? I guess it was just a way of getting Mickey to back off. Heck, I didn't need a matchmaker. I was no charity case. I was perfectly capable of managing my own love life. I just needed to work up the courage to talk to a girl. If I could manage to do that, all my problems would be solved. You see, once you're able to talk to a member of the opposite sex in a casual, informal way, then everything else just falls into place. You can start up conversations about homework or the weather or which teacher you hated the most. Then, when they realized you weren't some loser, you could naturally work up to the tougher questions. You can't just blurt out, "Hey, you wouldn't want to go out with me, would you?" It didn't work like that. You needed to ease into it.

And if that day ever came, I knew exactly what I'd do. I'd make a beeline for Andrea Walker, Andie to her friends, and if things went as planned—the future Mrs. Paulie Passero. There, take that, Mickey.

Chapter 2

All right, cards on the table. I'd had my eyes on Andie Walker for months. I stared at her in class. I listened in on her conversations. I sat across from her at lunch. I even followed her home one day. Now don't get me wrong. I'm not a stalker or anything, but when you've finally identified your soulmate, what are you supposed to do? Ignore it? Fight the urges? Hell, no. You have to act on them. Unfortunately, because I was a coward, acting on those urges usually meant just hanging around the girl of my dreams but never telling anyone what I was doing, especially her.

Andie was about three inches shorter than me. And thank God for that. I may not have mentioned it before, but besides the Roman nose, I'm also a little on the short side. Not short short, mind you. More like 5'7" short. I blame my parents. My mom is five feet three inches tall and my dad is five six, and shrinking. I never had a chance. So when you find a girl you can't get out of your head, and she doesn't tower over you, then you're onto something. The Mick never teased me about my height. And he could have. He was 6'1" in his stocking feet. It never was a big deal except when we played one-on-one basketball. He would always shoot layups. I, on the other hand, resorted to fifteen-foot jump shots. As you might guess, I was on the losing end most of the time. I suppose it explains why very few Italians ever made it to the NBA.

Oh, well, enough of that. Back to Andie. She had this shoulder-length, auburn brown hair. It was shiny and it smelled great. I was fortunate enough to be seated behind her at a school assembly one time. I kept dropping my pencil so I'd have an excuse to lean forward and smell her hair. And she was a jock. She was on the tennis team. I would always try to attend the home matches whenever I could. I didn't want Andie to see me sitting in the bleachers, so I would stand behind this metal fence and peek through. I don't think she ever knew I was there. As a matter of fact, I don't think she even knew I was alive. I needed to work on that.

So, my secret's out. But I'm not telling anyone else—especially Mickey. If he knew I had it bad for Andie, he would feel it was his responsibility to create a love connection. I wasn't ready for that. But I hoped someday I'd have the guts to start up a conversation with her. I didn't know if that was ever going to happen. One thing I worried about was if she started dating someone and they became an item. That would kill me. It was bad enough seeing her laughing and joking with some of the guys. To think that someone other than me would end up becoming her boyfriend was just too painful to consider. I kept telling myself if I didn't make my move soon, someone else would beat me to the punch.

I can't tell you how many times I found myself fantasizing about being her steady boyfriend. Now that would be so amazing. And I'd be a great boyfriend, let me tell you. I would always remember her birthday, and the anniversary of our first date, and Christmas, and Easter, and even Sweetest Day. I would shower her with gifts—or as many as I could afford on a stock boy's salary.

I'd been working as a stock boy at the High-Low Foods Market for the past year. As soon as I turned sixteen, I joined the ranks of the working stiffs. It wasn't like I wanted to or anything, but my dad put an end to my weekly allowance on my sixteenth birthday. It kind of sucked. If I wanted a little spending money in my pocket, then I'd have to be the one generating income. No more handouts. Having a part-time job was good and bad. The money helped. And it was kind of cool to tell other kids you had a real paying job. The bad part was actually having to do the work. And it tended to interfere with homework. I'd usually get scheduled for a five-to-nine pm shift on two or three school nights, and then again on Saturday afternoons.

Tonight was one of my few nights off. I spent the last couple of hours just lying on my bed and listening to the radio. My favorite was the Big 890—WLS. They had the best deejays, especially Art Roberts. I remember lying there and nearly dozing off when I heard my parents talking about something downstairs in the living room. I decided to eavesdrop on their conversation. I tiptoed down about four stairs and made sure I was still out of sight. Then I gently lowered myself onto one of the carpeted steps.

"I'm still not sure I should be going," my dad said.

"I think you should," my mother replied.

They had to be talking about the trip to Pennsylvania. I peeked out just enough to see my dad pacing from one end of the living room to the other.

"I don't know if she'll want to see me," he said. "Hell, I'm not sure she'll even recognize me."

"Oh, Peter, what are you talking about?" my mom said. "She won't recognize her own son?"

I listened for a few more minutes. It appeared my dad was having second thoughts about the trip. Now that was what I called great news. Maybe I could get out of going. The last thing I wanted to do was drive six hundred miles to some dinky little hick town. To appreciate the dynamic of what was happening here, you're going to need a little backstory. So here goes. My dad grew up in a traditional Italian family in central Pennsylvania. How my grandparents ever ended up in the little town of Leroy smack dab in the middle of the Alleghenies, I'll never know. I had always thought when Italians came to the U.S., they naturally settled in big cities like New York or Chicago. I'll have to ask my dad someday about how they ended up in rural PA.

Although my dad's parents had come to America decades ago, they only spoke Italian in their home. I remember my dad telling me one time that when he started first grade, he couldn't speak a word of English. He had never learned it. The other kids at school would make fun of him and use Italian slurs. It took him a while, but he eventually learned the language. And if you were to talk to him today, you would never pick up any hint of an accent. He could speak Italian like a native son one minute, and then have a conversation with you in English the next. I had always thought it would be pretty neat to know a second language. So why then with two years of high school Spanish under my belt did I remember only one word—*albondigas*—which meant *meatballs*. I supposed I could thank my alter ego—Mr. Underachiever. I wasn't dumb, but I was a little lazy. I had to admit it.

Well, fast forward to World War II. Following Pearl Harbor, my dad and tons of other guys enlisted in the armed forces. It was just what you did back then. My dad ended up in the Army, and eventually made staff sergeant. One time when he was stationed at a base in northern Illinois, he was told to go pick up an AWOL soldier in Chicago who had just up and left one day and returned home. It was on that mission my parents met. My dad had decided to visit a family that had lived near him in Pennsylvania when he was growing up. They had recently relocated to the Little Italy neighborhood in Chicago. During the visit, the family introduced him to the girl who lived upstairs—and the rest is history.

They fell in love and got married when my dad got out of the service. But they couldn't agree on where to live. My mom naturally wanted to stay in the Chicagoland area, close to her family and friends. My dad, on the other hand, felt he had to return to Pennsylvania to help run my grandparents' business—a local tavern. When my dad weighed his options, he realized Chicago was not only a better job market, but a location with better schools for when he and my mom had a family. To say the least, my grandparents in Pennsylvania did not take the news well. My grandmother greeted my dad with some especially harsh words. She told him if he moved to Chicago, he was no longer her son, and no longer welcome in her home.

That was more than twenty years ago. My dad hadn't spoken to his parents since then. He would occasionally converse with his siblings. My dad was one of four children. His older brother, Dominick, was killed in the Battle of the Bulge in Belgium in December of 1944 during the second World War. He didn't talk much about Uncle Dom, but I had heard him say on more than one occasion he would like someday to return to Leroy so he could visit Dominick's grave.

He also had a younger sister, Gloria. They apparently weren't very close. She still lived in their old hometown. She was a waitress at a local diner. I had never met her, and so I didn't know a lot about her. I did know she was divorced. One time when my parents didn't know I was listening, I heard them talking about her. They said Gloria had gotten married to her high school sweetheart the day before he was shipped overseas. He had apparently been injured by a land mine while in France. I remember my dad saying something like *she eventually left him because of it*. I always thought that was a crummy thing to do. Whatever happened to *for better or worse*? Maybe the guy was in a wheelchair or something? You're gonna divorce him because of that? I wanted to know more about it, but I couldn't ask my parents because they would have known I was eavesdropping.

Then there was his little brother, Fabrizio. Everybody just called him Buddy. Uncle Buddy to me. He was the only relative on my dad's side I had ever spoken to. It couldn't have been more than a few times, though. Uncle Buddy would call every few years and update my dad on how things were back home with my grandparents.

I knew my dad loved his brother, but there was something that just wasn't right between them. Whenever anyone would bring up Uncle Buddy's name, my dad would just roll his eyes and look disgusted. I could never figure it out. In the few times I had talked to him, Uncle Buddy had been so nice to me. He really seemed interested in whatever I was doing. We could probably have talked on the phone for hours, but since it was a long-distance call, it was usually only for a couple of minutes. I always wanted to ask my dad what was going on between him and his little brother, but I never worked up the nerve.

It was Uncle Buddy who had called a couple of days earlier and told my dad that their mother was dying. That was why we were headed back to Leroy. I guess he just wanted to say goodbye.

Since my parents had moved their conversation to the kitchen and out of earshot, I decided to make an appearance to find out if the Pennsylvania trip was still on. When I entered the room, my folks immediately clammed up. I wasn't trying to interrupt their conversation. I was just hoping they would continue even though I was there.

"Paulie," my dad said, "when do you start back up at school?"

"Um…the Tuesday after Labor Day, I think. Why?"

My mom turned to my dad. "You should be back by then, don't you think?"

My dad nodded. He pulled out a chair and sat down at the table. "Paulie," he said. "Are you packed yet? We'll be leaving soon."

"I wasn't sure that this thing was still happening," I said.

"Why would you say that?" my mother said.

"Well…um…"

"Go pack," my dad said.

I was about to bust. I had to talk him out of this. I was not about to give up the last two weeks of summer vacation without a fight.

"Why do we have to do this anyway? I mean, isn't this the same woman who basically disowned you twenty-some years ago? You don't owe her anything."

My dad sighed. "I see," he said. "So, when you're my age, and you find out that your mother is dying, you don't plan on attending her funeral? Is that it?"

I glanced at my mom and then dropped my eyes. He was making me seem heartless. But this was different.

"That's not fair, Dad. It's not the same thing. She told you she never wanted to see you again."

"You're right. When I told my mother I was moving to Chicago, in 1946, she cut ties with me. I haven't spoken to her since. And every day, I'm sorry about that. I probably should have made more of an effort to make things right. But I was just as pig-headed as she was. And then as time went on, I got used to the situation."

"Peter, none of that was your fault," my mom said. "Your mother was being unreasonable." She put her hands on my dad's shoulders. Then she leaned over and kissed him on the cheek.

"Paulie," he said, "I don't expect you to understand. In time, you'll see that this was the right thing to do, and you'll be glad you were there with me."

"Dad, this is between you and your mother. It has nothing to do with me. Why do I have to go? And what am I supposed to do about my job?"

"You'll just have to ask for the time off, that's all," he said.

"But, Dad, they want you to give them a month's notice if you need a day off. The schedules are already made up."

My mom sighed. "Then they'll just have to redo the schedule."

"I don't want to have to tell Mr. Columbo I need the next couple of weeks off. He'll have a fit."

"What am I supposed to do, Paulie?" my dad said. "I can't drive the entire six hundred miles myself. Not with my back. I need you to spell me behind the wheel."

Wait a minute. Wait just a minute. He wanted me to go with him so I could help *drive*? Why didn't he say that in the first place? I had been wanting to drive on the expressways ever since I got my license, but my parents wouldn't let me. I couldn't believe this.

"So you're gonna let me drive on the highways," I said.

My dad just nodded. He looked at my mom and shrugged his shoulders. "You think you're a good enough driver so you won't end up killing the both of us?" he said.

It wasn't what you would call a vote of confidence, but I'd take it. "I can do it. I know I can."

"I'm sure you'll do just fine," my mom said.

This was perfect. I still couldn't believe it. I could barely contain myself.

"When do we leave?" I asked.

"The day after tomorrow," my dad said. "It'll take us about ten or eleven hours to make it there. So you've got to be well rested. Understand?"

"I'll hit the sack early tomorrow night," I said. "Dad, how long are we gonna be there?"

21

He stood. "A week or two? I just don't know. It depends on the health of your grandmother. But I'll get you back in time for school. Don't worry about that. You'd better tell Mr. Columbo you're gonna need a couple of weeks off."

"I'll get the time off. Don't worry."

"A minute ago, you were having a cow about Mr. Columbo's reaction," my mom said. "What changed?"

I tried to conceal my euphoria, but it was no use. "Being able to drive on the highway. What'd ya think?"

"They call them turnpikes out east," my dad said.

"What's the difference?" I asked.

"It costs money to drive on them."

Oh, well, I wouldn't be the one paying. This was gonna be great. Other than work, I had nothing going here for the next two weeks. I was gonna be bored out of my mind anyway, but I couldn't tell my parents that. This would be a nice way to wrap up the summer.

"That's about it," my mom said. "Don't you think you should start packing?"

I shot back upstairs, pulled a suitcase out of a hall closet, and got to work. I loaded it with shorts and socks and T-shirts and underwear. I was ready to go in less than a half hour. I set the suitcase near the door, hopped onto my bed, put my hands behind my head and stretched out. I tried to imagine what a small town in rural Pennsylvania would look like. Would it be all farmland? Would the roads be paved or just dirt? What would downtown Leroy be like? Did they even have a downtown? Would people know we were from the big city by the way we talked? All of these questions were swirling around in my head.

Based on how things had gone when my dad left

his parents years ago, I wondered what our reception would be like. Would my aunt and uncle be happy to see us? I didn't know what to expect. And what about my grandmother? Would she hold on until we got there? And if she did, would she still be mad at my dad, and would she hold it against me? My enthusiasm about accompanying my dad was starting to wane. But whenever I pictured myself behind the wheel of our '66 Chevy Bel Air, roaring down the highway at seventy-plus miles an hour, I couldn't do anything but smile.

Chapter 3

The night before we left, I laid out everything I would need for the morning—jeans, T-shirt, socks, clean underwear, and gym shoes. My dad had told me to set my alarm for five o'clock. As excited as I was about the driving opportunity, I was less than thrilled with the early wake-up call. Five a.m. wasn't the morning—it was the middle of the night as far as I was concerned. But I decided to be a good soldier and make the best of the situation.

I was a little nervous about being in close quarters with my dad for ten hours, though. In the past whenever we were together, there was little to no conversation. We just didn't have that much in common. I wasn't sure whose fault that was. I guessed I could try to be a little more talkative. I would just have to see how things worked out. Of course, there was always the radio to break the tension. I wondered if he'd let me listen to music—my kind of music. My dad always had a rule whenever we drove anywhere—the driver controls the radio. I didn't think I could stand listening to news or talk radio for ten hours. That would be brutal. I fluffed up my pillow and slipped into bed. The adventure was about to begin.

Before I knew what had happened, the alarm was beeping. The dial read five o'clock. At first I just lay there shell-shocked. Then I realized morning was upon us even though it was still dark outside. I could hear someone on the stairs.

"Paulie," my dad said is a low tone. "You up?"

"Yeah," I said. My voice was a little scratchy.

"Be downstairs in fifteen minutes. Your mom made us something for breakfast. We'll eat in the car. Get a move on."

I dragged myself out of bed and trudged into the bathroom. A few minutes later I was standing in the kitchen. Both of my parents were sitting at the table having coffee.

"Do you want something to drink?" my mom asked.

"It's too early for anything."

She reached over and pulled down a paper bag off the counter. "There are some egg sandwiches in here when you get hungry." She pointed to a thermos on the table. "And there's orange juice in there."

"Put your suitcase in the trunk," my dad said. He pointed to a cooler sitting near the back door. "And take that too. It has our lunch in it."

All I could think about was going back to sleep as soon as I got in the car. I dragged my suitcase out the back door, down the porch steps, and into the garage. I tossed it into the trunk next to my dad's. I returned for the cooler. I thought it might be a good idea to put it in the back seat so it'd be accessible if we were to get hungry while driving. When I got back to the kitchen, I had apparently interrupted my parents. They were hugging.

"I wish I could be there with you," my mom said. "It's just so crazy at the bank right now I can't get away."

"It's fine," my dad said. "I don't expect you to be there. These people are strangers to you. I don't even know if they'll be happy to see me. And if they're not, I don't want to put you through that." They hugged again.

My mom came over to me, leaned over, and whispered, "You have to be there for your dad, Paulie. Do you understand? He may be walking into a hornet's nest, and he's going to need an ally. Can you do that for him?"

"Sure," I said. The way my mom was talking made me a little nervous. Were these people going to be unfriendly? Did they all hate my dad or something? This thing with his mother was just too weird. I mean, what mother disowns her own son just because he moves away? There had to be something wrong with that woman. I guessed I was about to find out. I hugged my mom, headed into the garage, jumped into the passenger seat, and promptly fell asleep.

I didn't wake up until we were somewhere in Indiana. I saw a sign for Elkhart. I had no idea how long I had been asleep. I yawned and stretched.

"I didn't mean to sleep this long, Dad. I can take the wheel at any time."

"I'm still okay," he said. "We'll pull over at the next rest stop and you can spell me. That'll be in about thirty-five miles."

"Okay."

"Can you get that bag in the back seat—the one with the egg sandwiches?"

I reached over and grabbed it. I dug in and pulled out a sandwich that still felt warm. I unfolded the wax paper and handed a half sandwich to my dad. There was nothing like a fried egg sandwich with a little butter on the bread—homemade Italian bread with the hard crust, that is. That bread was a family favorite. Whenever we had company over, everyone would reach for the homemade bread. It was one of the first things we'd run out of at a big dinner. My mom was one of the few wives who still found time to bake. I would usually let the guests eat as much of it as they liked. I was used to seeing a plate of bread at almost every meal. It wasn't that big a deal to me. Now don't get me wrong—I liked it—especially when it was right out of the oven. But I always tried to talk my mom into buying American bread—Wonder Bread or Silvercup. Those breads were really soft—even the crust. Whenever I asked her to buy it, she would say, "Now why would you want store-bought bread when you have homemade bread anytime you want? Don't be silly." And that was the end of the conversation.

It was quiet in the car. The radio was off. I would have preferred having it on, but if I asked my dad, I knew we'd end up listening to some talk show about the upcoming election. The Republican National Convention had taken place last week. Richard Nixon and Spiro Agnew (whoever that was) had been nominated. The Democratic Convention was set to take place next week. It would be held in Chicago. I wasn't sure if we'd be back for it or not. All I knew was the news radio stations were full of politics these days. Personally I found it all deathly boring. I supposed I should have been more interested in a presidential election, but for some reason, I just wasn't.

As I chowed down my egg sandwich, I looked out the window. The sky was overcast, which was fine with me. I preferred driving when the sun wasn't out. No squinting. The traffic was relatively light. For miles and miles all you could see was farmland. Corn and soybeans and whatever. People complained about all the congestion in the cities. All they had to do was relocate out here. There was plenty of room for everyone.

"That rest stop's coming up," my dad said. "You ready for a pit stop and then an hour or two of driving?"

"I'm ready."

We pulled into the rest stop a couple of minutes later. There was something neat about those places. When I was younger, I used to like seeing how many different license plates I could find in the parking lot. Now that I was approaching manhood, those things didn't really interest me. I was concentrating on getting behind that wheel and showing my stuff. I was a little nervous about having my dad riding shotgun. He was a real backseat driver. He could find something wrong with every move you made. Hopefully, he would doze off, and as Greyhound put it, he'd leave the driving to me.

After we freshened up at the rest stop, I hopped into the driver's seat. I planned to do everything correctly so my dad wouldn't critique me for the next hundred miles. I had actually spent very little time with him in the car when I was learning to drive. My mom handled all of that. And thank God. He was a basket case when he rode with a new driver. After I had gotten my permit, a few months back, my dad would occasionally offer to take me out on the roads. Each time it proved to be a disaster. "Slow down." "Speed up." "Put your turn signal on." "Don't follow so closely." "Come to a complete stop." "Stay in your lane." "Move over before you hit that car." It was the absolute worst. And from the passenger seat, he kept pounding his foot into the floorboard as if he were hitting the brake. He made me so nervous. I could only hope he had learned to relax. I was hoping for the best, but I was prepared for anything. I took a deep breath, buckled my seat belt, adjusted the rearview mirror, put the car into reverse, and slowly backed out of the parking space.

"The toughest part of highway driving is merging," my dad said. "Let's see how you do."

Merging. I hated merging, always worrying if someone was going to let you in. And if no one did, would you end up riding the shoulder? I never knew if I should speed up or slow down. But once I got into my lane, I would be fine. I began to accelerate as we pulled out of the parking lot and onto the entrance ramp. *Please, please, help there be an opening I can slip into.* I looked over my left shoulder. I put on my turn signal. There were three or four cars in the right lane. I wasn't sure what to do. Should I gun it and try to beat them? Or should I ease up on the accelerator and slide in after the last one had passed? I couldn't decide. A moment later I knew I had waited too long. I was now in no man's land. I couldn't squeeze in between them, and I was running out of ramp. I was hoping—praying—for one of the cars to change lanes and let me in. But no one did. At the last moment with no way out, I slammed on the brakes and ended up stopped on the shoulder of the road.

I buried my head in the steering wheel, waiting for my dad to explode. He was bound to take the wheel back and forbid me to drive for the remainder of the trip. But when I glanced over at him, he was just looking out the window with this blank stare. It was as if he hadn't seen what had happened. He never said a word. I decided to correct my blunder ASAP. I waited for an opening in the right lane, hit the accelerator, and merged successfully. I got up to sixty-five mph and pretended nothing had happened.

I snuck another peek at my dad. He wasn't paying attention to me at all. I wondered if he was all right. He put his head back, let out a long sigh, and closed his eyes. I couldn't figure it out. Why hadn't he gone berserk? It just wasn't like him. And then it hit me. He was thinking about something else—like what was awaiting him when he returned to his parents' home after more than two decades. Would he be welcomed back with open arms? Or would he be treated like a stranger? He had to have been wondering about that when I had my little merging fiasco. It was the only explanation.

I decided to enjoy my time in the driver's seat. I tried to relax, but it was difficult. Within a few miles, however, the tightness in my arms eased and I could just drive. This was going to be great. I hugged the right lane for the better part of the first hour, but when I got behind a semi going about fifty, I had a decision to make. There was something comforting about staying a couple of car lengths behind him and just coasting. But I didn't want to be in the car any longer than necessary. This drive would take us ten to eleven hours if we were doing the speed limit. I knew I needed to pass him. I waited until there was a wide opening in the middle lane, and then I put on my turn signal and made my move. And wouldn't you know it, just as I was trying to pass on the left, the semi sped up. Now he was doing 55...56...57. Why did this always happen? Why did people feel the need to speed up when someone was trying to pass them? It was so maddening. I leaned over and tried to sneak a peek at the truck driver. He seemed to be smiling. To him, this was a game. Well, two can play that game. The '66 Chevy Bel Air wasn't known as a muscle car, but when I floored it, the transmission responded nicely, and the trucker was soon eating my dust. There, take that.

Every mile on the road gave me more confidence in my driving abilities. What would make this an even better experience would be to have tunes on in the background. I thought about reaching over and just turning on the radio, but I was afraid of my dad's reaction. He might tell me to turn it off, or he might take over and look for some talk station. The more I thought about it, the more I wanted to go for it. I leaned over and grabbed the on/off knob on the radio.

"Dad, do you mind if I put the radio on?"

He turned from the window, faced straight ahead, and shook his head. Then he returned to watching the scenery, and reflecting, I guess.

I took that as my cue to find some jams. When I turned the radio on, I made sure to keep the volume at a conservative level. No reason to push things, since I had managed to get this far. When I flipped it on, the first thing we heard was some static. Then, with my eyes firmly fixed on the road, I began turning the knob to the right. The first station I landed on had someone giving what sounded like farm prices. No way. I kept turning. Next it was that boring elevator music. Forget that. Then it was an announcer who sounded kind of like a hayseed telling us about who had lost a pet in the area. Absolutely not. Next there was a newscast. And then finally, I hit pay dirt. Rock music. I left it on and waited for my dad to tell me to change the station. But he never did. Before he came out of his trance, two more hours had passed. We had crossed into another state. He rubbed his face and stretched.

"I didn't even notice we were in Ohio," he said.

"Yeah, about an hour ago," I said.

"So you think you've got the knack of this by now?"

"I feel like I've been doing it for years," I said.

"Don't get cocky. Bad things can happen to veteran drivers too. Just keep both eyes on the road and both hands on the wheel."

I nodded.

He looked at his watch. "Well, we can probably stop for lunch soon. Have you seen any signs for a rest area?"

"There's one in about five miles," I said.

"Okay, pull off when we get there." He sat back in his seat and stretched. "How we doing on gas?"

"It's between a half and a quarter."

"Okay, keep your eyes open for a station."

A few minutes later, I pulled off onto the exit ramp for the rest area.

"You can park up there by those picnic tables."

"Okay."

I pulled over and turned off the engine. We grabbed the bag of sandwiches from the cooler in the back seat and sat down at one of the tables. I picked the one in the shade. We didn't talk much during lunch. I knew my dad was in his own world right now. I was just thankful the trip had been relatively painless thus far. Good driving weather, although it was pretty hot. But what do you expect—it was August in Ohio. And my dad had been a pussycat. Couldn't ask for more.

A few minutes later, we were back on the road. My dad was behind the wheel now. I put my head back and closed my eyes. I found myself thinking of Andie Walker. I wondered what she was doing at that very moment. One thing for sure—she wasn't thinking about me. She had no reason to. I just hadn't made myself known to her. It wasn't for a lack of opportunity. Heck, I had seen her every day at lunch. But I just never built up the necessary courage to start up a conversation. I never knew what to talk about. I couldn't tell her I had watched her last eight tennis matches. It would sound like I was a stalker or something. And we hadn't had many classes together. I tried to imagine a more pleasant scenario—one where I said "Hi" to her, followed by a clever or funny line. But I never could come up with a clever or funny line. Oh, what was the use? Who was I fooling? I didn't have a chance in hell of ever ending up with someone like that. I took a long, deep breath and fell asleep.

Chapter 4

When I woke up we were entering Pennsylvania. We had stopped on the turnpike to pay tolls. My dad was waiting for his change.

"Okay, thanks," he told the toll booth operator.

"Dad," I said as we re-entered the traffic flow.

"Yeah."

I didn't know quite how to say it. I wanted to know what was waiting for us at my grandparents' home. I guess I just wanted to be prepared.

"What is it?" he said.

"I'm just...I'm just a little nervous about what it's going to be like when we get there. I mean—are people going to be happy to see us? No one even knows who I am."

My dad took a long breath. "Paulie, that's the sixty-four-thousand-dollar question. To be quite honest, I have no idea what kind of reception we're going to get. They could treat us like family. Then again, they could treat us like complete strangers. I just don't know."

"So, just how sick is my...my grandmother?"

"It's a little hard to spit that out, isn't it? Well, she *is* your grandmother, even though you've never met her." He looked over his shoulder to see if anyone was in the next lane so he could pass. "According to your Uncle Buddy, she's dying. She only has weeks, maybe only days, left. She has a rare form of cancer. I don't even know which kind."

"Will she be able to tell it's you?"

My dad shook his head. "I don't know. Buddy says she goes in and out of consciousness. I just hope seeing me doesn't make things worse. She was pretty angry the last time we spoke. And that was a long time ago."

I couldn't imagine not speaking to one of my parents for a few days, let alone two decades. It was so weird.

"And what about your father? Did he disown you too?"

My dad didn't answer right away. "Pop was...Pop was weak. He let my mom push him around. I think I probably could have stayed in touch with him as long as my mother didn't know about it. But I think he was too afraid of what she'd do if she ever found out. Buddy says he's slowed down a lot but is in relatively good health." My dad forced a smile. "He doesn't know you're named after him. I think he'll like that." My dad stared forward for a few seconds. I would bet he was thinking about his father. He was still smiling.

"It sounds like he might be happy to see us, don't you think?"

The smile faded. "I just don't know if she's poisoned him against me. I guess we'll find out soon enough."

"If you need a break, let me know," I said. "I don't mind taking the wheel again."

He glanced at the clock on the dashboard. "In a little while, maybe."

I wanted to know more about this side of the family, but I didn't know if or when my dad would get tired of all the questions. This may have been the longest conversation I'd ever had with my dad. And certainly the longest we had gone without an argument. Since things were going relatively well, and since he appeared to be in a talkative mood, I decided to press him.

"So will Aunt Gloria be there?"

He nodded. "Buddy says she's living with my parents now. She moved back in when your grandmother got sick."

"And you haven't talked to her in years either, right?"

He shook his head. "You know, I don't think Gloria really gave a rat's ass if I stayed or left town. You may have detected my sister and I weren't particularly close growing up. Gloria was always interested in—well, Gloria. She didn't have time for Dom or Buddy or me. She was always busy with her friends—mostly boys. She would move from one boyfriend to the next."

"She did get married, right?"

"Yep. But it didn't last long. When Norman came back from the war, she took one look at him and…" My dad stopped in mid-sentence. He had that look on his face like he had said something he wasn't supposed to. "Well, it ended." He stretched. "You're just full of questions today."

"I just want to be prepared for anything."

"Let's take a break for a little while."

"Okay." My dad had almost slipped with that Norman story. It had put a quick end to our conversation. I wasn't sure if I'd ever find out exactly what that was about, but the more he avoided talking about it, the more interested I was. I mean—if the guy came back a paraplegic or was shell-shocked or something, why couldn't he just tell me? I was old enough to understand. Anyway, it didn't make me think too highly of my aunt for turning her back on the guy.

I decided to give my dad the break he had requested. I reached into the back seat and pulled out a *MAD Magazine*. That would help me kill some time. There was nothing like following the exploits of good old Alfred E. Neuman.

My dad looked over and groaned. "Why do you have to read that crap anyway? Would it kill you to pick up one of the classics some time?"

"Dad, *MAD Magazine* is a classic." I knew that would start something, but I had to say it.

"Yeah, right." He shook his head. "You know, Paulie, if you spent a little more time with your school books rather than reading garbage like that, you might not be a C student."

Ooh, now that was a low blow. "I don't have any school books. It's still summer vacation."

"Would it kill you to read something like *Robin Hood* or *Huckleberry Finn* or *Treasure Island*? Now that's great literature. And it might even help you raise your GPA. You gotta think about impressing college admissions counselors. A 2.02 GPA isn't going to impress anyone."

It was time to set him straight. "Who said I'm going to college?"

He gripped the wheel tightly and locked his jaw. "I said. And your mother said."

"Dad, maybe I'm not cut out for college. You and mom are just high school grads and you're doing fine.

37

You're able to pay your bills, right?"

He sighed. "Life is more than being able to pay your bills. Your mother and I have *jobs*. We want you to have a *career*. And that's why you're going to college."

"So I have nothing to say about it?" Now I remembered why I avoided conversations with my dad. We always ended up arguing about something.

"Take your friend Mickey. He's planning on going to college."

"I'm not Mickey."

He was mumbling something under his breath. It was probably a good thing I couldn't hear him.

"Maybe your Uncle Buddy can talk some sense into you. He's a teacher, you know. A high school teacher. A high school literature teacher, to be exact."

"I didn't know that. So he has to have gone to college, right?"

"He went to St. Francis College in Loretto. It's not too far from Leroy. If you ask him about it, I'm sure he'll tell you what it was like."

I was really looking forward to seeing Uncle Buddy. He suddenly sounded more interesting to me than he had before. I supposed I could ask him about college, and I bet he wouldn't lecture me the way my dad did. I couldn't tell my dad I just wasn't smart enough to go to college. He would never accept that. And he was probably right. I knew I could do better if I only tried. But whenever I would talk myself into trying harder, I would somehow sabotage myself. I'd start missing assignments or not studying for exams. And I'd end up back where I started.

"There's a rest stop in a couple of miles," my dad

said. "We'll use the can and maybe you can drive for a little bit. I'll want to take the wheel back when we get off the turnpike. I think it's 146, the Altoona exit."

"Okay," I said. I was still kind of miffed at him, but I wanted to drive, so I had to at least appear civil. Ten minutes or so later, I was back in the driver's seat. The highway had gotten busier since the last time I drove. I really had to concentrate. I didn't want to screw up. Not at seventy miles an hour I didn't.

We drove for about ninety minutes with neither one of us saying a word. I wasn't sure when I'd get another chance to question my dad about Leroy. If I could manage to keep the conversation away from whether or not I'd be attending college, I thought I'd be relatively safe. There was one more family member I wanted to know something about. And this might be my only chance to find out.

"Dad, do you mind if I ask you one more question?"

He sighed. "Go ahead."

"Can you tell me something about my Uncle Dom?"

He shifted slightly to look out the window. When he turned back, he was smiling.

"Your Uncle Dominick was a real prince. He taught me everything, including English. Your grandparents only spoke Italian in the house when we were growing up. Dom would come home from school and complain to them about how the other kids made fun of him because he couldn't speak English. Pop spoke enough English to get by, running the tavern. I remember Dom spending a lot of time sitting at that bar. He wasn't drinking. He was trying to learn English from Pop's customers. I seem to remember some of the first words he learned were curse words. He liked to use them in front of your grandmother because she didn't know what they meant. It was pretty funny." He laughed.

It was unusual to see my dad laugh. I kind of liked it. He was always so serious.

"After the attack on Pearl Harbor, Dom was one of the first guys standing in line to enlist at the recruiting center. He was a real patriot. America—right or wrong. I remember when he got shipped overseas. He wasn't afraid. In fact, he couldn't wait to get into combat. He used to write these long letters about how it was such an honor to be fighting for our freedom. And he talked about the conditions over there. They were bad, but he never complained about them. Then one day the letters stopped coming. We waited weeks. And then we got a visit from a pair of Army officers. They handed us a telegram from the Secretary of War informing us Dominick—had been killed in action." My dad swallowed hard. He seemed to be fighting back tears. "He was a good man, your uncle." He turned to me. "We're going to visit his grave while we're there. I've been wanting to do that for the longest time. And I'm ashamed of myself it's taken me this long." He pulled a handkerchief from his back pocket and wiped his eyes.

I decided not to bother him for a while. He'd probably told me a lot more than he had intended to. I thought it best to just leave him alone for the time being. I had learned enough for now. The rest I'd have to pick up on my own. A half hour later, we saw the first sign for Altoona.

"That's the exit, Paulie. Once you get off the

highway, pull over. We'll switch places."

And twenty minutes later, my dad was back in the driver's seat. Once we were off the turnpike, we passed several farms. I could see cows and horses and even a few pigs. We weren't in Chicago anymore, that was for sure. There were one-pump gas stations, tobacco emporiums, Army surplus stores, and an occasional five-and-dime. The sun was getting low in the sky. I glanced at the clock on the dashboard. We'd been driving for about nine and a half hours. I was beat, and I was sure my dad was too. I was having a hard time keeping my eyes open. I thought about dozing off for a few minutes. Then my dad said something that kept me awake for the remainder of the trip.

"You might think this is silly, but I'm getting a little nervous."

I didn't know what to say. I had never thought of my dad as someone who got nervous. He was suddenly making *me* nervous. I found myself thinking about what my mom had said when we were leaving—I needed to be there for my dad because he might be walking into a hornet's nest. I decided at that moment I needed to man up and try to support him, even though I couldn't ever remember having to do so before.

"What are you nervous about?" I asked.

"The reaction from my parents and siblings," he said. "I really don't know what to expect. This could actually be a very short trip. I can't force myself on these people. If they want nothing to do with us, we'll just turn around and go home."

I didn't think he really meant it. You're not going to drive six hundred miles and then just turn around and do it again.

"Does anybody know we're coming?" I asked.

"Buddy knows. And he may have told the others. Or he may not have. He said he'd wait for the right time to break it to them. Who knows? Maybe there was no right time. This could end up being one hell of a surprise." He let out a long sigh. "I've prepared myself for the worst. But I don't want that for you. If they're not happy to see me, I hope they're at least civil to you. You haven't done anything wrong."

"Neither have you, Dad." I knew my mother would have wanted me to say that.

"Thanks for the support, but you may be a little biased," he said.

"If they don't want us around, well, I guess..." I tried to think of something clever, but all that came out was, "then I guess they don't want us around."

"We'll know pretty soon."

There wasn't much conversation for the rest of the trip. I killed time by looking out the window. What I saw made me a little depressed. There were a lot of rundown houses with paint peeling and broken windows and fences falling over and beater cars in gravel driveways. It appeared my parents had made the right decision twenty-plus years ago to leave the area. On one front lawn there was this bunch of kids with dirty faces and bare feet. They were poking each other with long sticks. One of the older kids must have seen me watching them as we passed by, and he gave me the one-finger salute.

Some of the storefronts weren't in much better shape than the residential areas. They had faded and crooked signs and weeds growing through the cracks in their parking lots. There were old men with canes sitting on benches and smoking cigars. There weren't many uplifting images on these streets. I suddenly found myself appreciating our house and neighborhood back home. I wondered what my life would have been like if my folks had never moved from here and I had grown up in this environment. Would I be one of those dirty, barefoot kids whacking my siblings with a stick? I couldn't ever remember thanking my parents for moving to Chicago and creating a better life for us. It wasn't the sort of thing a kid thinks about. But some of the sights in the last few minutes made me appreciate the things I had taken for granted all these years. I felt the urge to acknowledge it.

"Dad?"

"Yeah."

"I just wanted to say thank you for moving us out of this…" I wasn't sure what to call it.

"This hellhole?" he said.

"Well, I wouldn't have said it like that exactly."

"That's exactly what some of these towns have become. They're like zombies. They're dead but people stick around, and that makes them seem like they're still alive. But these folks are just going through the motions. It wasn't the place we wanted to raise a family."

And was I glad about that.

"Don't worry," he said. "We won't stay too long. We gotta get you back for school."

"That's okay," I said. "It wouldn't kill me to miss a few days."

My dad looked at me and rolled his eyes. He wasn't so dumb.

"We're getting close now," he said.

"How much longer?"

"Five minutes maybe."

Oh, boy. I wasn't sure if I was ready for this. I could feel my heart pounding right through my chest. My hands were getting clammy and my mouth was going dry.

I could only imagine what my dad was feeling at this very moment. It had to be even worse. I glanced over at him. His face was blank.

I suddenly felt bad for him. I tried to imagine having been disowned by my parents, and then showing up on their doorstep years later. I'm not sure I would ever have had the courage to do anything like this. My dad and I didn't always get along, but I couldn't help admiring him right now.

Chapter 5

We turned onto a road that looked like it had been frozen in time. If I hadn't known any better, I would have sworn it was 1948, not 1968. The houses looked nothing like the ones back home. Most were sorely in need of a new coat of paint. But that wouldn't have helped the dilapidated ones. I was starting to feel somewhat uneasy about making this trip. A minute later we came upon a sign that read *Leroy, Population 637*.

"It's right up here," my dad said.

I sat up in my seat and prepared myself for the unknown. We drove another mile and then pulled into a dirt parking lot.

"Well, that's it," he said. "And I'm happy, and sad, to say it hasn't changed a bit."

The house itself was enormous, but then I realized there was a tavern attached to it. A faded sign over the door said *Happy Time Lounge*. The condition of the place wasn't much different from any of the others. A handyman could have worked on the place for a month and it wouldn't have made much of a difference.

"Well, let's go do this," my dad said.

I looked at some of the other cars parked in the lot as I got out. Our '66 Chevy looked like a luxury car compared to them. I followed my dad to the front door of the tavern.

"I wonder if—" He stopped in mid-sentence. Then

he stepped back and crouched down. There was a welcome mat on the ground by the front door. My dad lifted the mat and underneath it was a key. "Some things never change," he said with a chuckle.

"What's that for?" I asked.

He nodded in the direction of the door. "It opens that door."

"Isn't it kind of dangerous leaving it out like that?" I said.

"You'd probably never do it in Chicago, but in Leroy, people are more trusting—or at least they were." He looked around. "I'll bet three-quarters of the people living in this town never lock their doors."

Our attention was suddenly diverted to the sound of a car with a nasty muffler problem. It was so loud you could barely hear yourself think. It came from the same direction we had just come from and roared up to us, heading on down the road. By now I could see it was an old pickup truck. There were people standing in the back of it. They looked like kids. Three boys and a girl. The boys were in dirty white T-shirts and jeans. And the girl—the girl was—I couldn't take my eyes off her. She had on a blue blouse, without sleeves, that was tied in a knot across her midriff—her bare midriff. And she had on these short, tight, cutoff jeans. She had dark hair that touched her shoulders and blew around in the breeze. She looked right at me for what seemed like several seconds. Then she ran her fingers through her hair and looked away. She was absolutely gorgeous.

My dad cleared his throat. I think he had figured out what I was looking at. "Um, let's go, Paulie." He pushed the door open. Thick smoke greeted us as we entered. A half dozen customers sat at the bar. Most appeared to be smoking and drinking beer. A few of them were wearing farm hats. The guy who was sitting closest to the door turned and eyed us suspiciously.

"Hey, Paul," he said, "did they change the drinking age in this place or something?"

A pudgy old man with thinning white hair and glasses looked up from behind the bar.

"What you talking about?" he said in a thick Italian accent.

The customer pointed at me.

The old man looked at my dad. "I'm sorry, sir. You can't bring that youngster in..." He stopped in mid-sentence and just stared at my dad for what seemed like an eternity. His face went white. "Peter? Is it you?"

"It's me, Pop."

The old man ran out from behind the bar as fast as his fleshy legs could carry him. He approached my dad and stopped. He put his hands to his face and began to cry. Then he threw his arms around him. He was saying something in Italian, but I couldn't understand it.

"Every day...every day I tell Mama someday Peter will walk through that door," he said. "I can't believe it's you. I am so happy."

"I am too, Pop," my dad said. He put his hand on my shoulder. "There's someone here I'd like you to meet. This is your grandson. His name is Paulie."

My grandfather looked up, tears streaming down his face. "Paulie? Paul?" he said to my dad.

My dad nodded.

The old man cupped my face in his hands and began to kiss me all over. I could feel the bristle from his beard on my cheek, and there was the smell of beer on his breath.

"We must celebrate. We must have a big party," my grandfather said. He stopped and placed his finger on his lips. The expression on his face turned sullen. "Oh, but Mama is sick. Very sick."

My dad put his arm around his father and led him back behind the bar.

"That's why I'm here," my dad said. "Buddy called me and told me about Mama."

My grandfather looked up. It was hard to believe, but he was actually shorter than my dad.

"Mama will be happy to see you, I think," he said.

My dad smiled. "Are you sure about that? She was pretty sore when I left. She said a lot of things that…"

The old man put his hand on my dad's mouth. "No, we don't talk about those things. You are home now. That's all that matters." He hugged my dad again.

From another room a woman appeared. She had on tight slacks and a low-cut blouse and a lot of makeup, and she wore her hair up. She looked at my dad and folded her arms.

"Well, if it ain't the prodigal son," she said.

My dad looked up and smiled. "Gloria. How have you been?"

They were standing two feet away from each other but neither made a move to hug the other.

"How have I been?" she said. "Lousy. I'm cooped up in here all day taking care of your mother. I had to take a leave of absence from my job. I'm barely making ends meet."

"I'm sorry to hear that."

"Don't be sorry," she said. "Pitch in, why don't you. I could use a break."

"Sure," my dad said.

She patted the back of her hair gently. "I'm wasting some of my best years playing nursemaid. I gotta get out and have some fun."

Most of my grandfather's customers had been listening in on the conversation. I supposed they found it pretty interesting. I sure did.

"Hey, Paul," one of them said holding his glass upside down. "This thing don't fill itself, you know."

"Sorry, sorry," my grandfather said. He took the glass, filled it up, and set it in front of the man.

"That's better," the man said. "Hey, Gloria, if you're looking for a good time tonight, I'm available."

She made a face. "You're married, Harold."

"That never stopped you before," he said.

All of the patrons started laughing. "That's for sure," one of them said.

Gloria, or rather my Aunt Gloria, waved him off and turned to my dad.

"Come on, I'll take you to her."

My dad and I followed her out of the bar, through a small room filled with—junk, I guess—which led into the kitchen.

Aunt Gloria held up her hands and waved them around. "Take a good look, Pete. Nothing's changed. Nothing ever changes around this place."

"Sometimes that's comforting," my dad said.

My aunt put her hand on her hip. "Bullshit. Boring is what it is."

She left the kitchen and walked into the dining room, where there was a set of stairs leading to the second floor. We followed her up the stairs and down a long hallway. She stopped in front of one of the bedrooms.

"She might not know you," my aunt said. "She's been unconsciousness for the last week and a half."

My dad nodded.

She opened the door and stopped. "If my memory serves me correct, you two didn't have a very pleasant conversation the last time you spoke." She smiled. "I'm gonna enjoy this."

My dad looked at her and grinned, but it wasn't what you'd call a happy grin. It was the kind of expression someone uses when they think the other person just made a smartass remark. I was now beginning to understand why my dad and his sister had never gotten along. She was just plain nasty.

She pushed the door open and stood aside.

"By the way, Gloria, not that you'd care, but this is my son, Paulie."

"Paulie? Cute. I bet the old man loved that," she said. "Well, it's nice to see the Passero name will live on—not that it matters."

I followed my dad into the room. Lying on her back, sleeping or unconscious or something, was my grandmother. Her hair was a mixture of gray and white, and she looked really old. Her face was full of wrinkles. My dad knelt down at the side of the bed and took her hand.

"Mom, Mom, can you hear me?"

"It's no use," my aunt said. "She's been dead to the world for days now. I don't know what she's holding on for."

"So you'd prefer it if she died...the sooner the better?" my dad said.

"Pete, she's full of cancer. If it doesn't kill her today, it's gonna kill her tomorrow, or the next day.

Don't make me out to be the bad guy. The sooner she goes, the less she'll have to suffer." She sighed. "And I can get my life back."

My dad leaned down and whispered something into my grandmother's ear. She didn't react in any way. It was a shame my dad had come all this way and his mother would never know it. She would never know he came back home to say goodbye.

My dad turned to his sister. "You don't have to stay here. We're fine."

She turned and walked to the door. "By the way, where are you staying?"

"We passed a hotel on our way in. That'll be fine."

"You don't have to play the martyr," she said. "You can stay in your old room, the one you and Dominick shared. It still has two double beds."

"Thanks, but we don't want to inconvenience you."

She made a face. "If you want to stay, you're welcome to. If not, then don't."

"Thanks."

Aunt Gloria sighed and left.

"Come here, Paulie. I want you to meet your grandmother."

I walked over and stood next to my dad. He motioned for me to sit down on the edge of the bed.

"Give me your hand," he said.

I held it out and he placed my grandmother's hand in mine. It felt rough and scaly.

"Sophia Elena Passero, meet your grandson, Paul Anthony Passero." He pressed our hands together and held them like that for a few seconds. It felt more like a few hours. I didn't know this woman, and what I did know, I didn't like. I wanted to pull my hand back in the worst way, but I didn't dare. This moment seemed very important to my dad. I'd just have to suffer through it. A minute or so later I was able to make my escape, at least as far as my hand was concerned.

I was still sitting on the bed. I wasn't sure what else my dad wanted me to do. I was hoping we would leave. We saw her. She couldn't see us. It was time to go.

"I know what you're probably thinking about this woman," he said. "But when I was growing up, she was a good mother. She never said it, but I always knew she loved me." He closed his eyes for a moment. "You know what she told me the night your mom and I were married?"

I shook my head.

"She said the only time you should tell your children you love them is when they're asleep." He smiled. "She was old school, Paulie. People raised their kids differently back then." He stood up. "Let's go get our stuff and bring it in."

"So we're staying here?"

My dad nodded. "Until they kick us out."

We went downstairs and out into the parking lot. We grabbed our suitcases from the car and brought them in. We re-climbed the stairs and walked down the long hallway. This time we passed my grandmother's room and went into another bedroom.

"It still looks the same," my dad said as he pushed open the door. He pointed to the bed closest to us. "That'll be yours. It was your Uncle Dominick's."

I wasn't so sure I wanted to sleep in a bed a dead guy used to sleep in, but I knew better than to say anything to my dad. The room itself was dark. There were these heavy drapes on each window. I walked over, pulled one of them back, and looked out. I was apparently looking out the back of the house. All I could see was thick brush and trees. Then I looked down. There was a relatively small backyard and then there was a huge drop-off. It had to be twenty or thirty feet.

"Dad, what's down there?"

He walked over to the window and looked out. "You'll have to go out there and see for yourself. At the bottom of that gulley, you'll find some old train tracks and a bunch of strawberries."

"Strawberries?"

"When we were kids, Dom and I would go down there and pick strawberries." He chuckled. "And occasionally we used to play chicken."

"What do you mean?" I asked.

"Don't ever do this. Whenever we'd hear the train whistle, we used to wait and see who could stay on the tracks the longest before jumping off and scrambling up the hill. We used to drive that engineer crazy. He would curse at us and tell us one of these days we wouldn't be so lucky." He smiled. "You don't have to worry. The railroad discontinued that route." He thought to himself for a minute. "I wonder if there are still strawberries down there."

I was learning things about my dad I was having a hard time believing. Was this the same guy who came home from work each night and barely talked to anyone, including my mom? There was something about this place that made him act differently. He had smiled and laughed more in the last twelve hours than he had in the last six months. But one thing confused me. The man had two brothers. So why did he only talk about one of them? I decided to find out.

"Dad?"

"Yeah."

"You talk about all these things you used to do with Uncle Dom. Didn't you ever hang out with Uncle Buddy?"

He sat down on the bed. "Paulie, you have to understand Dom and I were pretty close in age. Buddy was a few years younger. And, to tell you the truth, we didn't have that much in common. Buddy wasn't into sports, or anything physical, for that matter. He always had his nose in a book." He stopped and seemed to think about what he had just said. "I'm not saying it's bad to be studious. I wish a little of that would rub off on you. But you need to have balance in your life. There's time for books, and there's time for just being a boy." He stood up. "Let's go grab something to eat."

"Here?"

"No, I doubt there's much in the refrigerator. We'll go into town."

We went downstairs and informed Aunt Gloria we were going out for a bite to eat. My dad invited her to come along. She politely declined. So we hopped in the car and drove for about five minutes. It didn't take long to get to downtown Leroy, and there weren't many choices of places to eat. There only appeared to be two diners in town. We stopped at the one marked *Wilma's Restaurant*.

A waitress met us at the front door. "Sit anywhere you want," she said.

We basically had our pick of the joint. There were open booths everywhere. The next hour was relatively pleasant. We made light conversation of how the town had changed, or rather how it hadn't. I ordered a roast beef sandwich and fries. My dad had the meatloaf supreme. I tried my best to seem interested in what my dad was saying, but I kept thinking about that girl in the green pickup. I wanted to see her again, but I wasn't sure who she was or where she had come from. I needed to find out her name. I wondered if she had a boyfriend. And then I thought to myself, how could a girl who looks like that be unattached? It was impossible.

My dad tapped his fork on the table. "Paulie, did you hear what I just said?"

"Oh, sorry." I was thinking about something else.

He shook his head disgustedly. A few minutes later, after we had finished up and the waitress cleared the table, she asked us if we wanted dessert. *You don't even have to ask, ma'am.* I already knew the answer. In the handful of times I had been to a restaurant with my dad, he had always passed on dessert. When you were married to a woman who was the best baker in town, there was always something sweet to eat back home. And, I had to admit, it was outstanding. I had started to get up when my dad shocked the crap right out of me.

"Yeah, let's see the dessert menu," he said.

Hurry! Someone find my real dad and bring him back. On the other hand, I kind of liked this one better. I had a feeling, though, once we got home the real Peter Passero would return, so I decided to just enjoy it while it lasted. My dad ordered a piece of Dutch Apple Pie, and I enjoyed a hot fudge sundae. It was excellent. Twenty minutes later, we were back in the car, headed to my grandparents' home again.

I decided to restart the conversation. "Dad, are we gonna see Uncle Buddy tonight? Are you gonna call him and let him know we're here?"

"No, it's getting late. We'll see him tomorrow."

We were back at the Happy Time Lounge a few minutes later.

"I'm going to head into the bar and help your grandfather close up. You wanna come with?"

"Sure," I said.

When we walked into the bar, we found the decibel level quite high. There were about a dozen people sitting at the bar. Most had beers sitting in front of them. A couple had mixed drinks. My dad went behind the bar, where my grandfather was standing at the cash register with a confused look on his face. My dad motioned for me to sit at one of the empty stools.

"Pop, what's the problem?"

"I'm not sure of how much change to give him."

"Who?"

He pointed at a customer at the end of the bar.

"Well, how much did he have to drink?" my dad asked.

"I forget," my grandfather said. He was holding a five-dollar bill in his hand.

My dad walked to the end of the bar and said something to the customer in question. He returned, opened the cash register, made change, and returned it to the customer.

"It's all taken care of, Pop," he said. "Why don't you call it a night. Go get some sleep. I'll close up."

"Are you sure?" my grandfather said.

My dad nodded. "Paulie, why don't you take your grandfather upstairs, and both of you can hit the sack."

Hit the sack? What was going on? The last time my dad had told me to go to bed was when I was twelve. I was an adult now. *I* decided when it was time for bed. To be perfectly honest, I wanted to be there when something exciting happened. This was my first time in a bar. I wanted it to be memorable. I had to convince my dad to let me stay here.

"How about this, Dad? I'll take Grandpa upstairs and then I'll come back down for a few minutes. What do you say?"

My dad tilted his head and crossed his arms. "Nice try, son." He pointed to the door leading out of the bar. "Out! You're not even supposed to be in here. I'll be up in a little while."

I had known I'd never talk him out of it, but it was worth a try. I followed my grandfather out of the bar and through the kitchen. He climbed the stairs slowly and was out of breath when he reached the landing. He exhaled, smiled, held my head in his hands and kissed me on the forehead.

"Buona notte, Paolo." He disappeared into the bedroom where we had seen my grandmother earlier in the day.

I went into what I later discovered had been called the boys' room years ago. I got undressed and plopped into the bed Uncle Dominick had used. I put my hands behind my head and thought about all the new things I had seen and heard about today. There was my dying grandmother. It appeared as though I would never get to know her. I would have to rely on memories from my dad. My grandfather was a trip. A nice old man who didn't have a whole lotta backbone. But that was okay. I still liked him. Then there was Aunt Gloria. She was a whole different kind of trip. She was one unpleasant lady. I couldn't believe how matter-of-fact she was when she saw my dad for the first time in years. No hugs. No kisses. Just attitude. And that left us with the town of Leroy. Kind of a depressed area, if you asked me. How could my grandmother have expected my dad to make a living here? The town was brutal.

I closed my eyes, let out a long sigh, and within seconds, I was in full snooze mode.

Chapter 6

When I woke up the next morning, I could hear my dad snoring. That may have been what woke me up. I glanced at the alarm clock on the nightstand. It read 8:32. I hopped out of bed, grabbed some clean clothes from my suitcase, and hustled into the bathroom. Within ten minutes, I was headed downstairs. I found my grandfather sitting at the kitchen table, pouring a clear liquid into his coffee. The label on the bottle read *Anisette*. My grandfather must have seen me staring at it.

"It's like sugar but with a kick," he said with a smile. "Would you like some?"

"I don't think so," I said.

"You wait right there," he said as he got up, walked over to a cabinet, and returned with a mug. He set it down in front of me. Then he went over to the stove and brought back a coffeepot. He poured some into the cup. "You like coffee?"

"I guess I'm about to find out."

"I've been drinking coffee since I was a little boy," he said. "Just try it. You'll like it."

The smell was strong. I brought the cup to my lips and sipped. I made a face. It was so bitter, I couldn't believe it.

My grandfather laughed. "Now try it with this," he said as he poured some Anisette into the mug.

I sipped again. It was actually better. It wasn't so bitter anymore.

59

"So what do you think?" he asked.

"It's a little better," I said.

He picked up the bottle of Anisette and poured more of it into the cup. "Now try."

I sipped again. Whoa! It was really strong now. I could feel a burning sensation traveling down my throat and into my stomach.

"That's how you drink coffee," my grandfather said.

A voice from the doorway interrupted our conversation. "What are you two up to?" It was my dad.

"I'm just showing the boy how to make a good cup of coffee."

My dad's eyes went from the coffee cup to the bottle of Anisette and over to me. He walked over, picked up my cup, and smelled it. Then he took a taste and rolled his eyes. He walked over to the sink and poured it down the drain.

"Pietro," my grandfather said. "Now what did you do that for?"

"Pop, he's sixteen. He can't have alcohol. What were you thinking?"

My grandfather shook his head. "You weren't much more than five or six when you had your first glass of vino."

My dad looked away. "It was different back then."

"Why was it different? Why can't the boy have the same things you had when you were his age?"

The two of them continued arguing the merits and demerits of alcohol in a child's life. To tell you the truth, my dad had come to my rescue by disposing of the contents of that nasty brew. If I had had a chance, I would have done the same thing. My stomach was queasy from just a few sips. Whoever could handle that combination had to have an iron stomach. And that sure wasn't me.

On the other hand, we were dealing with a perfect double standard here. It was the old "Do as I say, not as I do" excuse. How could my dad rob me of this rite of passage? He was drinking when he was a kid. Why did I have to wait five more years to experiment with alcohol? It didn't seem fair, but I wasn't going to make a big deal out of it. How come kids always seem to want what they can't have even if they don't really want it?

My dad opened the refrigerator, took out a carton of eggs, and looked at the date. "Still good," he said as he glanced at me. "Scrambled eggs?"

I nodded.

My grandfather was still defending my right to imbibe. I wasn't really sure I wanted him to win this battle. I wanted to have the permission to drink alcohol, but not actually have to drink it. Does that make any sense? Finally, when he got tired of arguing, my grandfather waved his hand at my dad in disgust and left the kitchen. And then something I wasn't expecting happened. My dad let me have it.

"Paulie, what's wrong with you? We've talked about drinking before. When you're 21, I can't stop you. But I'll sure as hell do so until then. Couldn't you just say, 'No thanks,' to your grandfather?"

"Dad, I didn't know what he was putting in there. I didn't know it was alcohol."

My dad gave me one of those looks. "You didn't know it was alcohol? After the first sip, you couldn't tell?"

"Well, I guess I kind of knew then—but I didn't want to hurt his feelings. It's like he really wanted me to taste it."

"And so how *did* it taste?" he said.

"Pretty bad. I didn't want to drink it, but I didn't know what he'd say if I wasted it."

My dad broke four eggs into a glass bowl. "I don't want to have this conversation again. Do you understand?"

I sighed. "Yes."

Neither of us spoke at breakfast. I still had a bunch of Leroy questions for my dad, but now was not a good time to ask them. When I was done, I cleaned up after myself and drifted into the bar. It was closed. There was a sign on the wall that said it opened at four p.m. and closed at midnight.

I wandered into a large room off the bar. It had a shiny wooden floor with tables and chairs around the edges. The middle of the room was empty. I wasn't sure what it was for. On one end was this long table. Well, it sure looked like a table, but when I got closer to it, I saw markings on both ends. Then I realized it was a shuffleboard table. But where were the things you were supposed to slide down it? I went over to one end and found these heavy, circular, metal things with felt on the bottom. They were sitting in like a well at the end of the table. I picked up one of the weights and slid it down the table. It managed to go only about halfway. I needed more oomph.

"You're never going to beat anybody with a throw like that." My dad had come into the room. I guess we were on speaking terms again.

"You didn't tell me they had a shuffleboard table."

"I had almost forgotten about it," he said.

I held up one of the weights. "Dad, what are these called?"

My dad walked over to the table. "There are different names for them, but we always referred to them as *pucks*. You know, like in hockey. They're about the same size."

I pointed to the lines and numbers on the table. "What are these?"

"Those are the number of points you get if your puck lands in that space. But remember, you're tossing it the distance of the table. And your opponent is trying to knock your pucks off the table and into the alley."

"Got time for a game?" I wasn't sure how he would respond.

He checked his watch. "Okay, I have a few minutes before I have to look in on your grandmother."

"So how do we start?" I asked.

He moved in next to me at the end of the table and started separating the pucks. They were red or blue on top and silver on the sides. My dad pushed the red ones over to me.

"You can start," he said. "Just slide it down and try to get it as close to the edge as you can without it falling off. That way you'll get the most points."

"Okay, here goes." Remembering my weak effort a few minutes earlier, I pushed the first puck as hard as I could. It definitely went past the halfway point. Actually, it went flying off the end of the table and into the alley.

"Too much juice," my dad said. He slid his down about three-quarters of the way. He made a face. "No guts."

We continued to take turns until all eight of the pucks had been used up. Then we walked to the other end of the table.

"One of yours is hanging off the edge of the table," I said.

"That's called a hanger," my dad said. "It's worth four points."

"Oh, man, I need to get one of those." At the end of the first round, my dad was up five to two. We continued to play for the next several minutes. I never did manage to get a hanger. When all was said and done, my dad had beaten me fifteen to eight. But it was fine, since I had never played before and my dad had grown up with the game. He had the advantage…for the time being.

"Better luck next time," he said. "I'd better go check on your grandmother. I have to relieve your Aunt Gloria and I had better not be late, if you know what I mean." He smiled.

"Dad, one quick thing. What is this room used for? It can't just be for shuffleboard. Why all the tables and the open space in the middle?"

"That's a long story I'll try to condense. This room wasn't always here. Years ago, Dominick and I convinced your grandfather that if we could hold dances here, then the bar would attract more customers. He agreed. So he took out a loan and built this dance hall onto the bar. At first, everything was great. On Friday and Saturday nights, the place was packed. Everybody was happy. Then one night a fight broke out. I went to try to break it up when one of the combatants took the bottle of beer he was holding and broke it on one of the tables. He was still holding the bottle by its neck when he came after me with it. And at that very moment, your grandmother walked into the bar and saw what was happening. She was so afraid and angry she banned further dances at the bar. Dom and I tried to convince her this was an isolated incident, but she wouldn't listen."

"What did Grandpa do? Didn't he have a say?"

"Your grandmother set the rules in the family. Pop would never have had the guts to cross her. And so that was the end of the dances, and this room just collects dust now."

"Too bad," I said.

"It *was* too bad," my dad said as he glanced at the clock over the bar. "I gotta go." He pointed at the shuffleboard table. "Practice up, why don't you. We'll have a rematch later." And with that, he was off.

I will practice, I thought. *And next time I won't be such an easy mark. I'll give him a real game.* I slid all eight pucks down to the other side, then did it again and again. I was so engrossed in the game I didn't notice a man walk into the bar.

"You have got to be Paulie," he said.

I looked up. The man was standing with his hands on his hips and smiling. It was a nice smile. He was thin, with tight jeans, a short-sleeve collared shirt, and penny loafers.

"Hello," I said.

"You don't know me, do you?" he said.

I shook my head. I was slightly embarrassed I hadn't recognized him. Should I have? I wondered.

"I'm Fabrizio. Fabrizio Passero."

I still wasn't sure who this was. Apparently the look on my face suggested as much.

"I'm Buddy, Paulie. Uncle Buddy."

I could feel myself smiling.

He threw his arms out and walked over to me. Then he hugged me. It was a really tight hug. He pulled back and grinned.

"I am so delighted to meet you," he said. "Although we're not really meeting for the first time. We've spoken a few times on the phone. But I feel like I've known you all your life."

"It's nice to meet you too," I said.

"C'mon," he said. "We need to get to know one another." I followed him out the front door of the bar, across the front of the house, and up onto a covered porch on the side. There was an old-fashioned swing hanging by chains from the ceiling. Uncle Buddy sat down and patted the seat next to him. "Join me," he said.

I sat down, and he immediately started rocking the swing back and forth.

"I find I do some of my best thinking on this swing," he said. "I've solved the world's problems from right here."

I smiled.

"Okay, from the top. First, how old are you now?" he said.

"Sixteen."

He sat there for a few seconds and stared out into space. "Sixteen. That's a good age. Of course, it wasn't too pleasant for me, but that's a story for another time." He patted his lap with both hands. "So let me guess. You're going into your junior year in high school? Am I right?"

"Yep."

"I teach juniors and seniors. Did your dad tell you I'm a high school English teacher?"

"He did," I said.

"I was working on a lesson plan before I came over. We start up in a couple of weeks. You too?"

"Uh-huh."

"Are you excited about the new school year?" he said.

"Well…yeah…sure…you know." Not a good move on my part. I was talking to a teacher, and I wasn't sounding overly enthusiastic about school.

Uncle Buddy smiled. "And I quote…'Nothing great was ever achieved without enthusiasm.' Ralph Waldo Emerson…from his essay entitled 'Circles' in 1841. If you haven't figured it out, I'm an Emerson devotee."

I smiled and nodded. "Very nice." I mean—what else do you say after someone tells you something like that.

"Paulie, you're patronizing me," he said.

I wasn't sure what he meant exactly.

"What Emerson is saying is if you don't enter this school year with unbridled optimism and enthusiasm, how can you expect to succeed. Enthusiasm begets success." He waited until our eyes met. "Do you know what I'm trying to say?"

"Yeah, I think I do."

"So, bottom line—do you like school?"

"Sure," I said.

"Good, I'm glad to hear that. Have you started thinking about colleges yet?"

"Oh, yeah, I've given that a lot of thought." Yeah, right. I couldn't believe I was lying to this man. I had wanted to meet Uncle Buddy for the longest time. He was always so easy to talk to on the phone. I had been waiting for a chance to talk to him in person.

And so here was my big chance, and I didn't have the guts to tell him the truth. But what could I do? He went to college. He was a teacher.

I couldn't tell him I was a below-average student with little hope of getting into college.

"What schools have you thought about?" he said.

I knew I should have anticipated that question. I wasn't sure what to say, so I just blurted out the names of colleges in Illinois.

"Well, I'm thinking about Northwestern and the University of Chicago."

"Whoa, it's tough to get into those schools," he said. "Why am I lecturing you about success? You must be pretty strong academically."

"I do okay."

"Now you're just being modest," he said. "Let me tell you—I am so glad you take your studies seriously. Education is so important. I certainly wish I had more students like you in my classes."

I shrugged. I wanted this charade to be over, but I had only myself to blame. Couldn't we talk about something else? I wasn't sure how much longer I could fool him. And it wasn't like I wanted to or anything. I had just gotten in over my head. We needed to change the subject—and quickly.

"So how's your mom?" he said. "I always liked her."

Thank God, a new topic. "Oh, she's fine."

"I remember when your dad brought her to Leroy for the first time. It was culture shock is what it was.

Nothing like the big city. But your mom was a trooper. She never said a word when she learned we didn't have indoor plumbing and she'd have to use the outhouse."

Before our conversation could continue, I heard the same sound I had heard earlier—the pickup with the muffler problem. It was coming back the other way now. I focused on the bed, hoping for a glimpse of that great-looking girl. As it approached, it slowed down a little. There were still the three boys in the back, and standing up behind the cab, there she was. My eyes were glued to her. It seemed like she was looking right at me again as they passed. Boy, she was gorgeous.

"Hey, give him a little kiss, why don't you," one of the boys yelled out. He seemed to be aiming his jab at Uncle Buddy.

I could hear them laughing as the truck continued down the road.

"What was that kid talking about?" I asked.

"Oh, don't pay any attention to them," Uncle Buddy said. "They're up to no good."

But I wanted to know more about them, especially the girl. What was her name? How old was she? Did she come by here often? Where did she live? Did she have a boyfriend?

I wanted to know everything about her.

Uncle Buddy glanced at his watch. "I need to find your dad and say hello," he said. "You want to come inside or stay out here?"

"I think I'll stay here."

I sat back down on the swing as Uncle Buddy entered the house and found myself just staring into space, like I was in a trance of some kind, thinking about that girl.

We'd only be here for a few days. Would I ever see her again?

I had to.

I just had to.

Chapter 7

I sat on the swing for several minutes. I couldn't get her out of my head. I kept picturing her standing in the back of that pickup truck. I tried to think about what I would say to her if I ever saw her again. I couldn't think of anything. It was happening again. Why couldn't I talk to girls? What was wrong with me? It was so frustrating. I couldn't allow a beautiful girl like that to get away. I had to see her again. I would somehow think of something to say. I had to.

"Hey, Paolo," a voice said. It was my grandfather. He waved me over. He was carrying a large box full of trash. "Time to burn the garbage," he said. "You can help me."

As we walked down the road together, we passed an enormous garden that seemed to go forever.

"Whose garden is this?" I asked.

He laughed. "Who do you think? It is mine."

"You planted all this yourself?"

He smiled. "Of course," he said. "Who else would do it? Fabrizio is in school all the time, and Gloria is taking care of Mama."

This garden was huge. It had to be twenty-five yards by fifty yards. And it was loaded with stuff. I couldn't tell what some of the plants were. I did recognize corn stalks, although most of them were dry and brownish.

"I used to come down here every morning and pick some fresh Swiss chard. Your grandma made the best Swiss chard pizza. But now there's no one to make it."

"Not even Aunt Gloria?" I said.

He shook his head. "Gloria loved to eat it, but she never took the time to learn how to make it. Maybe if she had, she'd have a husband today."

I decided to avoid that topic. "Well, it's a great garden," I said. "And it's so big."

My grandfather chuckled. "Big? No, it's not big. You should see some of the farms around here."

"Are there any close by?" I asked.

"Sure, the Thompson farm." He pointed down the road. "See those trees down there?"

I nodded.

"There's a dirt road that goes for about a mile. Leads right to the Thompson farm."

"Maybe I'll take a hike down there and visit it sometime."

My grandfather threw his hands up. His expression had changed. "Absolutely not, Paolo. You can't go there by yourself."

"But why?"

He set the box of trash down on the road. "Thompson has these three sons who are bad, very bad. You wanna stay away from them. He brings them into the bar sometimes. Two of 'em aren't old enough to drink…but, boy, do they raise hell. I hate to see them come in."

I immediately thought about the pickup truck with the boys in the back. I wondered if they could possibly be the same family I had seen a little while ago.

"Does Mr. Thompson have a daughter, by any

chance?" I asked.

"He does—a girl about your age," he said. "Why do you ask?"

"When I was talking to Uncle Buddy a little while ago, I saw this green pickup with three boys and a girl in the back."

He picked up the box of trash and began walking again. "That was them." He stopped. "But like I said— you stay away from them. Okay?"

"Okay, Gramps."

He smiled. "It's nice to hear someone call me that. Gloria and Fabrizio don't have any little ones." He set the box down again and wrapped his arms around me. "I'm so happy you came to see me. I hope it's not another twenty years before I see you again."

"I don't think so." I didn't know for sure, but I couldn't imagine that happening. My dad's family, all except Aunt Gloria, seemed really happy to see him. I was sure he'd want to visit every so often. And I'd want to come along…as long as that girl was around.

I watched as Grandpa dumped the trash into a rusty old oil barrel at least four feet high. Then he pulled a box of matches from his pocket and lit a piece of newspaper. Within seconds, the trash was ablaze.

A minute later, we walked back up the road and into the house. Uncle Buddy and my dad were sitting at the kitchen table talking.

"Paulie," my dad said, "Buddy tells me you two already met."

I smiled. "Yeah."

"We chatted a little," Uncle Buddy said. "But we have a lot more to talk about. Right, Paulie?"

"Right."

"Paulie, Gloria left. I have to sit with your grandmother," my dad said. "I shouldn't have left her alone. Can you find something to do?"

"Sure," I said. All I really wanted to do, though, was learn more about this Thompson girl. I decided to question Uncle Buddy about the family. I sat down at the table just as my dad left.

"We could talk now if you like," I said.

Uncle Buddy patted the table with both hands. "Works for me. So what should we talk about?"

"Um…how about those kids in the pickup truck that passed us a little while ago?"

Uncle Buddy pouted. "Oh, them." He forced a smile. "What do you want to know?"

"Well, grandpa said the boys are troublemakers."

"Troublemakers isn't the half of it. They're thieves and vandals and arsonists and *murderers*."

My jaw dropped.

Uncle Buddy pulled up his chair. "There's a farm next to theirs—belongs to the Lenharts. Those two families have been feuding for as long as I can remember. About a year ago, the Lenharts' barn mysteriously went up in flames. He lost some cows and horses. But the worst part was one of his farmhands, a Mexican fellow, was asleep in the barn when the fire started. He had burns on ninety percent of his body. He died a day later. The sheriff was convinced the Thompson boys were responsible, but he couldn't find enough evidence to charge them."

I wanted to ask him about their sister, but suddenly I wasn't sure if it was worth it. I had no interest in tangling with a group of psychos. But every time I closed my eyes, I could see her standing in the back of the pickup, running her fingers through her hair. I just had to know.

"Uncle Buddy?"

"Yeah."

"I was just wondering. That girl in the back of the pickup. Is she a problem child too?"

Uncle Buddy leaned back in his chair. "I was wondering when you'd ask about her." He smiled.

"Oh, I was just curious," I said. "But if you don't know, it's no big deal."

"No big deal, huh?" He chuckled. "Her name is Guinevere. I think they call her Guennie. I had a feeling you'd notice her. She's a very pretty girl. And the answer to your question is—I don't know if she gets into trouble, but I don't think so. Her name never seems to come up when her brothers get caught doing something."

"Do you know how old she is?"

Uncle Buddy put his finger to his lips. "I seem to remember seeing her at school as a freshman, but after that she just disappeared. She must have dropped out. That was about a year ago." He grinned. "That would make the two of you about the same age."

I nodded. "Well, thanks. I was just wondering."

He leaned over. "I'm sure you wouldn't mind running into her again. But the problem is those brothers of hers. I hear they're very protective. Paulie, I'm just not sure it's worth it. I'd hate to see you get hurt. After all, 'the first wealth is health.' Emerson again. From 'The Conduct of Life,' 1860. Anyway, those brothers of hers have scared off plenty of suitors for Guennie."

"Well, I don't plan on sticking my neck out for

anybody," I said. But I would—for her. And when I thought about seeing her again, or maybe even talking to her, suddenly those brothers of hers didn't scare me. I began to fantasize about it. I wanted to be alone with her. I wanted to touch her soft skin.

"Let's talk about something else," he said. "What was the last good book you read?"

I didn't even hear the question. I was somewhere else, trying to imagine a scenario when our paths would cross. What would I say to this mystery girl? It had to be really good. Not the same old drivel. I had to impress her. After all, I was from the big city. I was supposed to know my way around.

But I didn't know my way around. And I didn't know how to talk to a girl. What was it about girls that made me turn into mush whenever they were around? It was like I couldn't think straight.

Mickey was right. There was something unnatural about being sixteen years old and never having gone out on a date. It wasn't like I didn't want to or anything. I just couldn't pull the trigger. I couldn't start up a conversation with a girl to save my life. In a way I blame my parents. Why did I have to be an only child? Why didn't they have more kids? If I had had a sister, I would have gotten comfortable talking to girls. And that would have helped eliminate my awkwardness around them.

"Paulie? Paulie?" Uncle Buddy said.

"I'm sorry. I guess I wasn't paying attention."

"I wonder what you were thinking about—as if I didn't know," he said.

I could feel myself turning red. How did he know I was thinking about that girl? I needed to do a better job of hiding my emotions in the future. This was embarrassing.

Uncle Buddy put his arm around me. "Paulie, I was sixteen once. I know all about raging hormones. You don't have to be shy with me."

In a way I wanted to talk to him about it, but the only person I had ever had conversations about girls with was Mickey. I couldn't just blurt out mushy stuff. I barely knew the man.

"It's okay," he said. "When you're ready, you let me know. I won't pry. Just know you can always talk to me about anything. Got it?"

I nodded.

He looked at his watch. "Mail should be in any time now. I think I'll run over to the post office. Why don't you come with me. It'll give you a chance to see a little more of the town—what little there is to see."

"Sure," I said. What did I have to lose? I wasn't doing anything. I didn't have to be anywhere.

We hopped into his 1966 Chevy Corvair. This was a sweet ride, let me tell you. It had the gear shift on the dash and the engine in the rear. On the way *over town* (that was how Uncle Buddy referred to the busy section of town), he continued his probe of my love life, but I wasn't biting. As we drove I thought about how spoiled we were at home. A mailman stopped by the house six days a week. I couldn't imagine having to go to the post office every day to get the mail. But folks here just accepted it. There was something actually comforting about that. The pace was slower here. I could almost get used to it.

When we got closer to our destination, I noticed the same green pickup truck parked in front. The

Thompson boys were sitting in the back. They appeared to be smoking. There was an older man with a scraggly beard behind the wheel. Uncle Buddy spotted them right away. He pulled the car over about fifty yards from the post office.

"I think we'll just wait here until they leave. No sense to tempt fate."

But I wanted to tempt fate, especially if it meant a chance to see her—Guinevere.

"Why don't I go in there and pick up the mail," I said. "Does everybody have their own box? Do you need a key?"

"I don't want you going in there. We'll wait here."

"I don't mind," I said. "I'll be fine."

Uncle Buddy glanced at me. He had that look on his face like he knew exactly why I was volunteering.

"Okay," he said. "But be careful. All you have to do is ask the man behind the desk for the mail for Buddy Passero and Paul Passero. If he asks any questions—and he might since he used to be family—just tell him you're Paul's grandson and you're visiting from out of town. Okay?"

"Okay." I jumped out of the car. I didn't want to miss an opportunity to see her one more time.

Uncle Buddy reached over and rolled down the passenger side window. "Remember what I said. Just steer clear of those boys."

I nodded. I headed directly for the post office, but then at the last minute, I decided to make a slight detour. I walked over to a butcher shop a few doors down and made my way from the opposite direction. I was hoping the Thompson group wouldn't notice me. But just as I reached the front door of the post office, one of them popped up.

"Hey, stupid," he said.

I looked up. Big mistake.

"So you answer to 'stupid,' huh? That must be your name."

I didn't say a word. I kept my head down and turned away.

"Hey, stupid, I'm talking to you."

I pushed open the post office front door. It slammed behind me. I didn't know what they had in store for me when I went back out there. I decided to wait inside until the truck pulled away. When I looked up, I spotted her immediately. She was standing by the front desk. There was a glass window separating her from a man on the other side. I waited for her to turn around. Of course, I knew I'd never have the guts to say anything. But I just wanted to get a good look at her face. The man behind the glass pushed a stack of mail in her direction.

"Here you go, Guennie," he said.

She didn't say a word. When she turned toward the door to leave, I caught a quick glimpse of her face. It was the face of a goddess. She looked at me for a few seconds. I knew it wasn't polite to stare, but I couldn't take my eyes off her. I knew I should have looked away, but I just couldn't. She was the most beautiful creature I had ever seen. And it was that natural beauty. She wasn't wearing a stitch of makeup. It made me think of Violet from my bus rides to school. I wondered if Violet would look as good without makeup. I was guessing she wouldn't.

So Uncle Buddy was right. They called her Guennie. I could hear myself calling her by name. I could picture us having a conversation. But this was not the time or place for that. I needed to get up the nerve. And I was nowhere near that. When she turned away, I couldn't help but notice her skin. It was beautifully tanned and looked so soft and perfect. I could feel my heart racing. As she grabbed the door handle, someone pushed it open from the other side. It was one of her brothers—the one who had ragged me when I came in.

"How long does it take you to pick up some mail, stupid?" he said.

I wasn't sure if he was talking to me or his sister. When I looked over, he had his hands on his hips and was staring a hole right through me.

"Are you talking to me?" I asked. I thought politeness might help me finagle my way out of this.

"Who do you think I'm talking to? The door?" He moved toward me.

I backed up a few steps. I wasn't sure where this was going. I should point out I'm no fighter. I had made it through two years of high school without ever having been beaten up by an upperclassman. I wanted to maintain that record.

He looked at Guennie, then back at me. "Oh, I see what you're up to. Well, let me tell you something, pal. You had better just get your filthy eyes off of my sister or I'll kick your ass right here."

"What are you talking about, Johnny? He didn't do anything," Guennie said.

She was actually sticking up for me. This was great. Before I knew it, however, her brother was in my face. He was poking his finger in my chest—pretty hard, actually. Guennie tried to pull him away.

"Let's just get outa here," she said.

"Not before I teach this punk a lesson," he said.

He pushed me up against the wall and raised his arm. But before he could connect, the man who had been standing behind the glass came out of a door a few feet away and grabbed Johnny's arm.

"I told you I don't want you boys in here," the man said. He pointed at Guennie. "She's fine, but the rest of you stay the hell out."

"And how do you s'pose you're gonna keep us out?" Johnny said.

The man walked over to the door he had come out of, reached in, and pulled out a shotgun.

"This'll do all the talkin' for me," he said. "Now get out!"

Johnny made a face and pulled the door open so hard the Venetian blind that was hanging on it came flying off. He shot through the opening and disappeared. Guennie bent down to pick up the blinds.

"Leave that, Guennie. I'll take care of it," the man said.

"I'm sorry about all this, Norman," she said. "He just gets so crazy sometimes."

"It's all right."

She turned toward me as she was leaving. She looked at me kind of funny. It wasn't a smile or a frown. It was more of a blank stare. Maybe I shouldn't have, but I took that as a good sign. A moment later, she pulled the door closed behind her. I looked out the window and saw her climb into the back of the pickup and say something to her brother. Then it pulled away.

"What did you need, son?" the man asked.

"Um…" I had suddenly forgotten why I had come in there.

"Are you picking up mail, or do you need stamps, or are you mailing something?"

I thought to myself for a minute and finally got my bearings. "I need to pick up the mail for Buddy and Paul Passero."

The man smiled. "Are you related to them?"

"Yeah. My name's Paulie. Buddy's my uncle and Paul is my grandfather."

"Wait a minute. Wait just a minute. Are you...Peter's son?"

I nodded.

"Is he back in town?" the man asked.

"Yes."

He shook his head. "Well, I'll be. I'm going to have to stop by and say hello. Of course, I'd better wait until Gloria's not around. We don't quite see eye to eye."

"Oh?" I said.

"We were almost related, you and me. I used to be married to your Aunt Gloria. But that was a long time ago." He stopped and seemed to be thinking to himself for a minute. "Well, I'd better get that mail for you." He went through the door that led into the back room and showed up behind the glass at the front counter a few moments later. "Here you go, son." He pushed a stack of mail toward me.

"Thanks," I said. I made my way to the door but stopped short. I suddenly felt the need to say something. "Mister?"

"Yeah."

"Thanks for...well, you know."

"That little dust-up with the Thompson boy?"

I nodded.

"I'd advise you to steer clear of those boys. I've banned them from the post office. So you be smart and keep your distance. Understand?"

"I understand." I turned to leave.

"And tell your dad Norman says hi."

"I'll do that. Thanks."

Chapter 8

When I got back to Uncle Buddy's car, he was a nervous wreck. "What happened in there?" he asked. "Why did it take you so long? Are you all right?"

"I'm fine."

"I saw one of those boys go in there. Did he bother you?"

"Well, he would have if Norman hadn't stepped in."

"Oh, so you met Norman, huh? He used to be your uncle. Did he tell you that?"

I nodded.

"He's a good guy," Uncle Buddy said. "Too bad things didn't work out."

I wanted to ask Uncle Buddy a question about that, but I wasn't sure if I should. I remembered my dad saying Aunt Gloria divorced her husband after he had been injured in the war. He said she had left him because of the injury. I'd just figured he was in a wheel chair or something. But he looked perfectly healthy to me. He was definitely able to handle himself when that Thompson kid showed up. I decided to ask and take my chances.

"Uncle Buddy?"

"Yeah."

"Why did they get divorced? Aunt Gloria and Norman?"

He put his hands in his lap and stared forward for a few seconds without speaking.

"Well, I guess you're old enough to know," he said.

I wanted to hear his answer, but I was a little nervous about having asked. Maybe I was prying. Maybe I had crossed over some line I wasn't supposed to. Suddenly I was sorry I had asked.

"Norman was hit by shrapnel after someone in his regiment stepped on a land mine in France. The metal lodged in a part of his body that..." He stopped and seemed to struggle with how to phrase things. "It hit him right..." He sighed. Uncle Buddy turned to me. "Paulie, the injury left him unable to perform in bed. He wasn't able to...you know, and that unfortunately was the reason your aunt wanted out of the marriage. It makes the words *in sickness and in health* seem pretty empty."

So that was it. That was the reason. He wasn't a cripple. He hadn't come back from the war in a wheelchair. He was able to perform *almost* all of the functions a man needs to perform. It seemed kind of selfish of Aunt Gloria to have pulled out of the marriage over that. But who am I to say. I hadn't lived it. I wasn't the one who'd have to make the sacrifice. But I like to think if something like that had ever happened to me, I sure hoped my wife wouldn't walk out on me.

"Can I ask one more question?"

"You can ask as many questions as you like," he said.

"Did Norman ever find anyone? Did he ever get married?"

85

"Now that's a story with a happy ending. He *did* get married...to a wonderful gal. She was someone who was able to look beyond his incapacities and love him for the person he was."

"I assume they didn't have any kids."

"Another happy story. They adopted a boy and a girl a few years after they got married. The boy is working in Pittsburgh, I think. And the girl's at Penn State."

"I'm glad."

"Me too. In a way I'm kind of glad about the divorce. He was too good for Gloria. She would have screwed that up and made him crazy." He shrugged. "Hey, can I take a look at that mail in your lap?"

"Oh, sorry." I handed him the stack of letters.

He began sifting through them. "Bill, bill, bill...oh, what's the use." He set the mail down on the seat between us and glanced at his watch. "Ooh, I have an appointment in a half hour, but I think we have enough time. Want to see my place?"

"Sure." It didn't take more than a few minutes to get there. We ended up at a trailer park on the outskirts of town. We pulled off the main road and followed a dirt road past some pretty sad-looking trailers before we stopped at a bright yellow one. It had flower boxes at each window. It definitely stood out from the rest.

"Well, there she is," he said. "Home sweet home. Come on in and take a look."

I followed Uncle Buddy up a couple of steps and into what he called home. Once I crossed the threshold, I was actually surprised at how much room there was. You almost felt as if you were in a real house. You walked into the living room, which had a couch, chair, ottoman, and a TV. To the left was a hallway that led to a bedroom and bathroom. To the right was the kitchen. For one person, it seemed adequate.

"This is a pretty nice trailer," I said.

"We prefer to call it a *mobile home*." He chuckled. "On a teacher's salary, it's the best I can do, but it's comfortable."

"It's great," I said.

"Well, back to the hearth," he said. "Let's go."

We drove back to my grandparents' home where he dropped me off. For the remainder of the day, things were fairly subdued. Uncle Buddy had an appointment somewhere. And Aunt Gloria still hadn't spoken word one to me since I had gotten there. It was as if I was invisible or something. But it was actually perfectly fine with me. I didn't have anything to say to her either. The bar was quiet. A few regulars popped in, but it wasn't what you'd call a festive atmosphere. Everybody pretty much just sat and quietly nursed their beers. I sat on the edge of the shuffleboard table and watched some TV for a while. The channels came in kind of fuzzy but there wasn't much I could do about it. The reception was really crummy. The closest station we could pick up was CBS out of Altoona. There was a lot of snow in that picture on the screen.

I hit the sack early that night. Before I drifted off, I found myself thinking about Guinevere. I had to think of some way to see her again. I thought about traveling down the dirt road at the end of the hill and seeing if I could catch a glimpse of her. I needed to do so without attracting the attention of her brothers, though. I had no intention of tangling with them again. There wouldn't be anybody there to protect me. The more I thought about it, the more I knew I had to do it. Against everyone's advice, I made a plan to try and find her the next day. If I never saw her again, if I never talked to her, it would haunt me for the rest of my life. I had to do this.

****

I woke up to find my dad, fully dressed, standing in front of the window, just peering out. He turned around as I sat up in bed.

"What day is it?" he asked.

"Wednesday, I think."

"How long have we been here?"

"A couple days, I guess."

"It's like time stands still around this place. When you don't have a job to go to or a family to come home to, you lose track of time."

I knew exactly what he meant. I was having a hard time remembering what day it was myself.

He stretched. "So what's on your agenda today?"

"Not much. I thought I'd just poke around here a little. I might try and see if I can find my way to the post office. It seemed like it was walking distance."

"It's about a mile and a half," my dad said. "Listen, I'm sorry I don't have time to show you around this place. I want to stay close to home in case your grandmother…well, you know."

"Don't worry about it, Dad. And can you let me know when you're ready to visit Uncle Dom's grave? I'd like to go with."

He smiled. "And I want you to come—when the time is right. I'm just not ready to deal with that yet. I'm afraid it's going to be pretty emotional. But we'll definitely get there before we leave." He turned towards the door but stopped short. "Listen, I'm going to run out and pick up a few groceries. I assume you'll be okay."

"I'll be fine." I jumped out of bed, got cleaned up, and headed downstairs for some breakfast. Like before, my grandfather was enjoying a cup of coffee with a little anisette. No, thanks.

"Good morning," I said.

"Buon giorno, Paolo. That's how you say good morning...*buon giorno.*"

"Buon giorno," I said. I kind of butchered it.

He clapped. "Very good." He reached over and took my hand. I hadn't noticed before, but the pointer finger on his right hand was cut off at the first joint. It was kind of creepy. I slowly pulled my hand back, but I kept staring at his finger.

He held it up. "You're wondering about this?"

"Yeah."

"It happened about forty years ago...when I was working in the coal mines. They used to have these little railroad cars that traveled on a track deep down in the mines. An empty car would come along and we'd fill it up with coal. And if we didn't finish quickly enough and send it on its way, the next car would arrive, and it would crash into the first one. I made the mistake of having my hand on the handle of the first car as the second one smashed into it. It tore the end of my finger right off."

I cringed. I couldn't imagine having something like that happen. I wondered what his finger looked like after the accident. The whole thing creeped me out. A moment later, my Aunt Gloria appeared. She looked tired and didn't seem to be in the best mood. Was she ever?

"Paulie, is it?"

Was she talking to me? "Um…yeah."

"Go keep an eye on your grandmother for a few minutes until your dad comes back. I need a break."

Wait a minute. That wasn't my job. At least, I didn't think it was. But how could I say no? I only hoped my dad wouldn't be long.

"Can you go now, please," she said.

"Gloria, the boy hasn't had his breakfast," my grandfather said.

"And I haven't had a good night's sleep in weeks. It's not gonna kill him, Pop."

"I'll do it," I said. "I don't mind."

Aunt Gloria forced a smile. "It won't be long. Come and get me if she soils herself."

Oh, now that was a pleasant thought. I climbed the stairs to the bedroom level. When I got to my grandmother's room, I knocked lightly. I wasn't really expecting to hear her voice, but I just thought I should. A moment later I pushed her bedroom door open and entered. She was lying on her back, as usual. Her breathing was a bit labored. I pulled up a chair and sat down next to her.

I watched as her chest moved up and down ever so slightly. The covers were nearly up to her neck. I looked around the room as I sat there. I hadn't noticed it when we were in this room earlier, but there were statues of saints all over—on the dresser, on the nightstand, on the windowsills, and on the chest of drawers. I got up to check out a few of them. There were three of St. Anthony, two of St. Therese of Lisieux, four of St. Jude, and assorted others. I guess she just felt safer with all the saints around her.

I sat back down and kept an eye on her for the next several minutes. I started to doze off, but I was abruptly awakened when she began coughing. I sat up. I wasn't sure what to do. She kept coughing. I waited for Aunt Gloria to come back in, but she never came. When my grandmother seemed to be losing her breath, I put my hand behind her head and lifted it up. That seemed to help. She got her breath back finally. I gently placed her head back on the pillow. It seemed like we were back to normal. At least, I hoped we were. Boy, that was scary.

But then a strange thing happened. She opened her eyes and turned her head to look at me. I stared back momentarily, then looked away. She lifted her hand and reached for mine. I extended my hand and grabbed hers. Her fingers were all bent. Should I say something, I wondered? Was she awake? Could she hear me? With her other hand, she motioned for me to come closer. When I did, I could just barely hear her speak.

"Who are you?" she whispered. "Are you with the doctor?"

"No," I said. "My name is Paulie. I'm your son's son. I mean—I'm your grandson."

Her eyes opened wider. "Are you Peter's boy?"

"Yes," I said with a smile.

She squeezed my hand. "Is he here?" Her voice was straining.

"Yeah, he's here. Not exactly. He's here in town. But he's not here right now. He went to the store."

"I knew he'd come back." She closed her eyes and a smile began to form on her lips. And then she was quiet again and back to the same state she had been in since we had gotten here. I couldn't wait to tell my dad we had talked. I knew he'd think it was so cool.

The door opened and Aunt Gloria walked in. "I'm back. Your shift's over," she said.

I got up to leave. I wasn't sure if I should tell her what happened. Would she want to know? Would she care? I was nearly out the door when I stopped.

"Aunt Gloria?" I said.

Her head snapped. "Well, that's the first time anyone ever called me that." She shook her head. "What is it?"

"I thought I should mention she woke up. We were talking."

"What are you saying?" she said. "This woman, here in this bed? She's never going to wake up. You must have been imagining it. You know, you shouldn't joke about something like that."

"Joke about what?" My dad had entered the room.

"Your son says Mom woke up and she was talking to him." She let out a laugh. "Looks like you raised a fibber, Peter."

"Paulie?" he said. "What happened?"

"Well, she started coughing, and I didn't know what to do. Then she started choking. So I lifted her head up, and it seemed to help. Then a few seconds later, she opened her eyes and grabbed my hand."

"You're serious?" he said.

"Yeah. Then she asked who I was, and I told her. Then she asked if you were around, and I said that you were at the store. Then she said, 'I knew he'd come back,' and she smiled. And then she was out again."

My dad shook his head. It appeared he was having a hard time believing my story.

"Sounds a little farfetched," he said. "Just like that, she woke up and started talking?"

"Yeah."

"You actually believe that hogwash?" Aunt Gloria said. I didn't appreciate her lack of support.

"Paulie, you shouldn't be toying with someone's emotions," my dad said. "Maybe you heard what you wanted to hear."

"Dad, it's the truth. She woke up and talked to me."

"Well, I'll never believe it," Aunt Gloria said. "The woman is near dead. Take it from me, she's never going to regain consciousness. You needed to be here a few weeks ago if you wanted to talk to her."

"I know you think this will make things better," my dad said to me, "but it only makes them worse. I'd rather have you say nothing at all than lie to me."

I didn't know how to convince him it had really happened.

"I think you should leave," he said.

This wasn't fair. I had told the truth. I shouldn't be treated like this. I needed to defend my position.

"Dad, I wouldn't lie about something like that."

He pointed to the door without even looking. I couldn't believe this was happening. I glanced at Aunt Gloria. She was smiling. She was apparently enjoying this little melodrama. If this were a movie, Grandma would wake up right now and start talking. That would show them. But it wasn't a movie. I left the room. Chalk up one more time my dad had shot me down.

Chapter 9

I was so angry at what had just happened in my grandmother's room I wanted to scream. It was so unfair. Just because I was a kid, I had to have been lying, is that it? At this point, I would never be able to convince them she had spoken to me. They would just have to find out for themselves. I took a deep breath and tried to calm down. I needed to refocus my energies. I needed a distraction to get my mind off this. It was time to change course and concentrate on more pressing matters. I didn't think anyone would miss me, so I made an executive decision right on the spot. I knew what I was about to do might seem reckless, but I decided to head in the direction of the Thompson farm. I ran outside and began following the paved road down the hill to the dirt path. I had to see Guennie again. I had been thinking about her constantly since the first moment I laid eyes on her. And seeing her was just what I needed at that very moment.

When I reached the dirt road, I looked back at my grandparents' home. I suddenly began to think about something Uncle Buddy had said. Was he right about her brothers setting a fire that took someone's life? Were they that dangerous? I knew they wouldn't hesitate about pushing me around the way one of them did at the post office, but exactly how physical would they get, I wondered. I didn't want to find out, but I needed to see her one more time. If Grandma passed away in the next day or two, they'd probably arrange a pretty quick funeral, and we'd be on the road within a couple of days. I didn't know how much time I had left, but I needed to make the most of it.

The path was lined with tall brush on both sides. I didn't know what any of the vegetation was. To me, they were all just big weeds. I glanced down and noticed tire tracks in the mud. They were too big for your average car. They had to have been made by a truck of some kind. It had to be the Thompsons' pickup. Sure. That was it. I plodded along for the next quarter hour fantasizing about what it would be like to be alone with Guennie.

A few minutes later I heard the sound of an engine. It got louder with every second that passed. I could tell it was coming from the direction I was headed. I knew, with all of the twists and turns on this dirt road, a car could be in your face before the driver ever spotted you. I decided to step into the bushes and hide there until the vehicle passed. Within a few seconds, the green pickup truck I had seen before flew by. An old man wearing a straw hat was behind the wheel, and three boys sat in the back. It was the Thompsons' truck, all right. I was sure of it. But I didn't see Guennie in the back. Could that mean she was alone at the farm? This might be my big chance.

I began to pick up the pace. I didn't know how much time I'd have before her dad and brothers returned. I continued to forge ahead along the dusty dirt path. I kept looking over my shoulder to see if anyone was coming. For the next five minutes or so, I must have sneezed twenty-five times. I apparently was allergic to some plant life in the area. But that wasn't about to stop me. About ten minutes later, I was able to make out an opening in the trees about a hundred yards ahead. That had to be it, I thought. Before long, I was staring at a dark red barn. There was a white house next to it with broken shutters and peeling paint. In the distance, I could see cows and pigs and chickens. There was a metal wire fence around all of it. I just stood there for a moment, taking it all in.

Then a couple of minutes later, I heard a sound coming from the barn. When I saw what it was, I crouched down behind some bushes to hide. It was Guennie riding a black horse without a saddle. She had on a white T-shirt and the same cutoff jeans. She was barefoot. She used her fingers as a comb and ran them through her hair. I couldn't stop staring at her. It was like I was in a trance. She was so beautiful. The whole time I was admiring her, I failed to notice she had turned the horse sharply and was headed in my direction. She was coming right at me. I crouched down even further and put my head down. Then there was a moment when everything stopped and I heard nothing.

"Come out of there, whoever you are," she said.

I froze. I didn't know what else to do.

"My dad has a gun in the house. Do you want me to get it?" she continued. She moved the horse closer to the bushes. "I can see you as plain as day. Come out of there right now."

I decided it was time to come clean. I stepped out from behind the bushes.

"It's you," she said. "You're the same kid who was in the post office, right?"

I nodded. I could tell my face was turning red. I

was so embarrassed. She had caught me spying on her. I wanted to run.

"So what are you, a peeping Tom or something?" she said.

I needed to think fast. "No, I was just taking a walk. That's all."

"In the bushes?"

"Well, I stopped there to rest for a minute."

She cocked her head and looked at me skeptically. "What's your name?"

"Um…Paulie…Paulie Passero."

She looked surprised. "Are you related to that family up the road?"

"Yeah, they're my grandparents."

Her eyes narrowed. "Well, listen, *Mister Paulie Passero*. This is private property here, and you are trespassing."

Now wait just a minute. I was suddenly building up a little courage. "You own that dirt road?"

She folded her arms. "Yeah, you got a problem with that?"

"Well, listen, Guennie…" Oops.

The look on her face stopped me in mid-sentence. She jumped down off the horse and began to march toward me. We were no more than a foot away from each other when she began waving her finger at me.

"Nobody, and I mean nobody, calls me that unless I tell them they can. You got it?"

"Sorry."

"You should be," she said.

I was getting some confidence back. "What can I call you, then?"

"Nothing! You can't call me anything! Just who do

you think you are anyway? And how do you know my name?"

I had to think quickly. I didn't want to say I had been talking about her with someone. That would seem creepy. And then I got this brainstorm.

"I heard Norman call you that at the post office."

She looked at me as if she were looking right through me. "What are you doing here?"

"I'm just visiting from Chicago. I'm not trying to cause any problems…really."

She flashed a sarcastic smile. "Chicago. Well that explains it. Are you trying to be one of those gangsters like Capone?"

I worked up a half smile. "That was eons ago. Chicago is nothing like that now."

"Not from what I hear," she said. "I've seen all those Edward G. Robinson movies. I know what it's like."

Before I had a chance to defend my hometown, she stopped and put her hand up. "Shhh," she said. She was trying to hear something. "Oh, no, it's them," she said.

"Who's them?"

"My dad and my brothers. And if they find you here, they'll kick the shit out of you for sure."

I dropped down behind a bush.

"Oh, they'll never find you there," she said sarcastically. "Hurry up." She reached down and lifted the bottom wire in the fence.

Was she inviting me in? I wasn't sure what to do.

"What are you waiting for?" she said. "You wanna get caught?"

I dropped down and slid under the fence.

"C'mon," she said.

I followed her into the red barn, which smelled awful. She pulled the barn door closed and began to look around.

"Follow me," she said. She raced over to a rickety, handmade wooden ladder, and started to climb it.

When she reached the top, I was still standing there.

"What are you waiting for?" she shrieked.

"Is that thing safe?" I said, pointing to the ladder.

She rolled her eyes. "Listen, kid, I don't know why the hell I'm sticking my neck out for you. I must be crazy." She shook her head. "Will you just get up here...please! If my old man finds us in here, he'll tan my ass for sure."

I didn't want that to happen. I didn't want anything to happen to her. I ran over to the ladder, gritted my teeth, and began the climb. With each step, the ladder creaked. When I was about halfway up, one of the rungs gave way, and I slipped down and nearly fell.

"C'mon!" she said.

I continued my ascent as quickly as I could. When I reached the top, she gave me her hand to pull me up. I didn't want to let go. It was so soft and warm. I noticed she had really short fingernails. It looked like she bit them.

"Let's get behind those," she said.

She pointed to several bales of hay, in the corner of the loft, that created a wall of sorts.

I ducked down and followed her. When we were safely behind the hay bales, she sat down Indian-style and motioned for me to join her.

"Thanks," I said.

"Well, I was wondering when you'd realize I was

saving your life," she said. She looked away disgustedly.

"I definitely appreciate it. I didn't really want to tangle with your brothers. They looked kind of tough."

"Tough? They're crazy is what they are. I can't tell you how many times they've kicked the crap out of the boys who've come here to see me."

"Oh, so you're pretty popular?"

She laughed. "Well, I was. Until my old man pulled me out of school. Now no one comes around."

"Wait, you mean your dad made you quit school?"

She appeared defensive. "Well, I wouldn't be the first one who did."

"What grade would you be in?"

"I should be a junior in high school in the fall. But that's never gonna happen."

"You can't just tell him you want to go back?"

She shook her head. "It doesn't work like that in this family. You go to school until you don't have to anymore, and then you quit and work the farm."

"Doesn't sound like much of a life," I said.

She sat up defiantly. "Oh, what makes your life so much better?"

I thought for a moment. I needed to come up with a really good answer. And then just as I was about to mount a defense, she put her hand on my arm.

"I heard something," she said.

There was definitely a sound directly below us. Someone was opening the barn door.

"Get down," she whispered.

You could hear footsteps on the barn floor. "Guennie. Guennie, are you in here?" It was a boy's voice. It had to be one of her brothers. "She's not in here," the voice said to a second person. "Where do you suppose that little slut is? She's supposed to be getting supper ready." Then the voice faded out.

What a jerk, I thought. Guennie was no slut. How could someone refer to his own sister that way? I peeked at her. Her eyes were closed. She rolled over onto her back and put a piece of hay in her mouth.

"Real nice, huh?" she said. She seemed a little embarrassed. "What I wouldn't give to get off this farm." She flipped back onto her stomach and rested on her elbows. "I'd start runnin' and I'd never stop." Then she suddenly sat up and pulled away from me. "I don't know why I'm telling you all this crap. I don't know you from a hole in wall." She got up and peeked over the edge of the loft. "When I think it's safe for you to leave, I'll come back. I still don't know why I'm doing this."

"Where are you going?" I said.

"Chores. I got chores to do, Einstein."

"But what if they come back?"

"Well, I guess we'll find out just what kind of a man you are, won't we?" She sighed and rolled her eyes. "Relax. They won't come up here looking for you."

"You can't stay just a little longer?"

"They're already lookin' for me. If I'm gone any longer, it'll turn out bad for both of us."

She climbed down the ladder. I got up and looked over the edge. She opened the door just enough to peek out. She looked up and saw me watching her.

"Get away from there. I'll be back when I can."

I returned to my cubbyhole behind the hay bales and relaxed—as much as I could. I was hungry, thirsty, and I had to go to the bathroom. I didn't know how much longer I'd be stuck up here. I figured I had been gone for a couple of hours. Right about now my dad would be looking for me. If I had to stay here much longer, he'd go through his ritual of first getting pissed and then starting to worry. I should probably start working on a good story to tell him. I couldn't tell him the truth about how I wanted to see this girl who I'd never met and didn't know anything about. He would think it was silly. Hadn't my dad ever been sixteen, with a body full of overactive hormones?

Then again maybe he would actually understand. Maybe I could tell him the truth about where I'd been. But the more I thought about it, the more I knew he would never understand. He wouldn't even try to. It was time to come up with a real whopper.

As I sat there with my brain going a mile a minute trying to think up an excuse for having been gone so long, I came to an amazing realization. I had just conquered one of my greatest fears and I hadn't even realized it. For years I had been unable to talk to the opposite sex. Every time I was with one of them, I would turn to mush. It was impossible for me to have a normal conversation with a girl no matter how hard I tried. But today, with Guennie, it was different. We had actually struck up a conversation. A lot of it was her yelling at me, but that wasn't bad for starters. I didn't just melt the way I had done so many other times. I was able to listen to what she said and was able to respond in a normal way. I wasn't trying to come up with something clever to say, I was just talking to her. I thought back and tried to figure out what I had done differently.

Before I could figure things out, both of my arms, at the same time, suddenly became really itchy. I looked down and noticed red splotches all over them. What the heck was going on? I began scratching them. But the more I scratched, the more itchy they got. I couldn't stop scratching. One area just below my elbow had gotten so red and raw it began to bleed. I knew I needed to stop scratching, but it was nearly impossible to stop. I sat there and fought the urge. It was really hard, let me tell you. I fell back onto the hay and lifted my arms away from my body. How long could I lie there and avoid the urge to scratch? I began counting to sixty to see how long I could make it.

The barn was hot and stuffy. I didn't know how long I'd be up here. I was sure Guennie was looking for an opportunity for me to escape. I closed my eyes, tried not to give in to scratching my arms, and fell asleep.

Chapter 10

When I woke up it was pitch black in the barn. I couldn't see a thing. I crawled over to a window. I could just make out the moon's reflection on a tractor at the edge of a field. That was all I could see. I wondered what time it was. I was thinking about my dad, and how pissed he probably was right about now. I figured I could handle him. I'd done it before. But I was more worried about how I was going to get back to my grandparents' house. There were no streetlights out here. How on earth would I find my way back?

Just then I heard something directly beneath where I was sitting. I rolled into a ball and held my breath. My greatest fear was that Guennie had told her brothers about me and they were coming up here to teach me a lesson. I could now clearly hear the door being slid open. I prayed it was Guennie and not someone else.

"Hey," a voice called out in a loud whisper. "Paulie Passero, you still up there?" It was Guennie.

I crawled out from behind the bales of hay and scurried up to the edge of the loft.

Guennie stood below with a flashlight in her hand. "Come on down. We gotta get you outa here."

I scooted over to where the ladder was and felt for the top rung with my foot. I then slowly and methodically made my way down. I had, of course, forgotten about the rung I had broken getting up there.

When I went to reach for it, I felt my foot dangling in the air. A moment later I slipped down the remainder of the ladder and hit the bottom with a thud. I was sitting on the barn floor with Guennie's flashlight shining in my eyes.

"Can you please move that thing," I said.

"Boy, you're real graceful," she said as she fought to keep from laughing.

When I got up, I noticed her studying my arms and shining the flashlight on them. "What happened to you?"

I began to scratch the affected areas. "I don't know, but they're really itchy."

She took a closer look and shook her head. "You dope. That's poison ivy. Those bushes out there are loaded with it. How could you be so dumb? Don't you know what poison ivy looks like?"

"I guess I don't. We don't have much of it where I come from."

"When you get back to your grandparents' house, you better put some cream or something on there."

"But how am I ever going to find my way back? I won't be able to see a thing."

She waved the flashlight. "With this. Just follow the dirt path until it turns into a paved road. Then you should know your way from there." She handed me the flashlight. "Now get out of here and don't come back."

But I had to come back. This couldn't be the last time I would ever see her. I then said something I had never said to any girl in my life. I don't know where I got the courage to say it, but it just came out.

"I want to see you again," I said.

She put her hands on her hips. "How many times

do I have to tell you? That's impossible. My brothers would do a real number on you. You go back to your life, and I'll go back to mine."

I didn't know why she was telling me this. Was it because she was worried about my safety? Or was it because she had no interest in seeing me again? I had to know.

"So, what happens when you want to see somebody? I mean—you must have had a boyfriend at one time."

She smiled. "I could have. But my sibs scared them all away. Now go...before it's too late."

I walked over to the barn door and stopped. "Thanks. I'll see you. And I really mean that."

"Sure. Sure. So long, Paulie Passero. It was nice knowing you."

I pointed the flashlight out the barn door and began moving it all around until I could see the bushes where I had entered the property. I ran over to the fence and barely managed to slide under the bottom wire where Guennie had let me in. I scraped my back on the barbs and ripped my shirt. I reached around to see how bad it was. When I put the flashlight on my hand, I could see blood. Great, now I had something else I'd need to explain.

I held the flashlight out in front of me as I navigated the dirt path. I was able to see where I was going, although I could tell the beam of light kept getting dimmer. That meant the batteries were starting to fail. I didn't know how much juice I had left. I began running to save time. I could hear a flapping sound overhead. I couldn't tell what it was. I assumed it was some kind of bird, but when the sound got louder and closer to me, I pointed the flashlight upward and caught a glimpse of the intruder.

Oh, my God, it was a bat!

I put one hand on my head and clutched the flashlight with the other. I ran as fast as my legs would carry me. I tried turning the flashlight off for a few seconds to conserve the power, but all I managed to do was lose my bearings and lurch headfirst into a pile of bushes. I dug myself out of the greenery, flipped the flashlight back on, and continued my trek up the dirt path.

I ran and I ran until my side ached. I stopped for a moment, caught my breath, and resumed the seemingly endless journey. The light was straining now. It would be out soon. I had to keep going. Sooner or later I'd stumble upon the paved road, although it seemed like that would never happen. I kept moving forward.

The flashlight was now worthless. I was about to pitch it but then I remembered it didn't belong to me. That's right. It was Guennie's. I needed to return it. That would give me an excuse to see her again.

I slipped the flashlight into my back pocket, held my hands out in front of me, and continued on. Without light of any kind, I was traveling without a rudder. I had no idea if I was going in the right direction. For all I knew, I could have been headed back to the Thompson farm.

The fluttering had stopped. Hopefully that meant the bats were gone. I heard a few hoots. Those had to be owls. They were harmless. Then I heard another sound that scared the crap out of me. It was a long, shrill howl. It seemed to be coming from the direction I was heading. Would I walk right into it? Would I come face to face with a coyote? I wasn't sure if they were dangerous or not. Were they more afraid of me than I was of them? I couldn't remember if I had ever read anything about them. I only knew about coyotes from what I had seen on *Bonanza* on Sunday nights. I didn't ever recall them attacking Ben or Hoss or Little Joe. I just had to hope they wouldn't bother me either. I said a prayer God would lead me in the right direction.

Minutes later I felt hard concrete under my feet, and in the distance there was a house with light coming from its windows. The moon briefly snuck out from behind a cloud, and I could see my grandfather's massive garden on my right. I had done it. I had found my way back. I let out a long sigh. I was exhausted. I dragged myself up the road to the house.

When I was within fifty yards of my destination, I stopped. Wait a minute, I thought. I needed a story. I needed something my dad would buy. He would probably be relieved to see me at first, but that would be short lived. I knew he'd eventually be upset. I had to come across as the victim of some plot Mother Nature had devised. I thought about it for a minute.

Okay. That might work. I had taken a walk down the dirt road and had gotten lost. Maybe I could throw in something about wild coyotes. I needed to sell it. My dad might not like it, but if I sounded so relieved to be back, he might just go for it.

I entered through the back porch, which led into the living room. I glanced at a clock on one of the end tables. It read 11:45 pm. Oh, God. I couldn't believe it was that late. This wasn't going to be pleasant. There was a light on in the kitchen. I could hear voices. It was time to meet my executioner. When I entered the room,

Uncle Buddy was the first one to see me.

"Oh, thank God," he said. He got up from the table and threw his arms around me. "Paulie, where have you been? We've been so worried about you."

"It's a long story," I said. I looked around for my dad. He wasn't there.

Aunt Gloria was sitting at the kitchen table drinking a cup of coffee. She didn't bother getting up.

"Where've you been, Cinderella?" she said as she looked at the clock. "Your coach was about to turn back into a pumpkin, you know."

"Is my dad around?"

"He's out there looking for you," Uncle Buddy said.

I made a face. That was not good.

"He should be back in a few minutes," Aunt Gloria said. "He said if he couldn't find you by midnight, he was going to call the sheriff."

Uncle Buddy studied my condition. "What happened to you?" He pointed to my arms. "What is that?"

"Looks like poison ivy to me," Aunt Gloria said. "I've got some cream upstairs that might help with the itching."

Uncle Buddy grabbed my shoulder and turned me around. "You're bleeding."

"I must have rubbed up against some bushes somewhere," I said.

"We need to get that shirt off you and put some iodine on those cuts," he said.

I heard the front door open. Here comes nothing, I thought.

When my dad entered the kitchen, his jaw dropped.

"Where the hell have you been? Do you have any idea what you put me through tonight?"

"I'm sorry, Dad."

"That's all you have to say?"

"It's a long story," I said.

"I'm listening…and it better be good."

I glanced at the three of them before I began. I was trying to figure out who my allies might be. Uncle Buddy looked concerned. My dad looked pissed. And Aunt Gloria just looked bored.

"I'm waiting," my dad said.

"Can I sit down?" I asked.

"No," my dad snapped.

"Peter, the boy looks exhausted," Uncle Buddy said. "Who knows what he's been through. Let him sit down…please."

My dad sighed and waved in the direction of a chair.

I sat down. *Okay, here goes.* "First of all, I'm really sorry about all of this. I never meant to be out this late. I didn't have a watch with me, so I didn't know what time it was or I would have been back sooner." That was a lie. It wouldn't have mattered if I were wearing a watch or not. I had been a prisoner in Guennie's barn with no means of escape. Oh, I supposed I could have taken a chance and made a run for it, but there was no way I wanted to tangle with her brothers.

"Okay, okay, you're sorry," my dad said impatiently. "But where have you been?"

"I…um…just took a walk down that dirt path. I just wanted to see where it led, that's all. I got a couple of miles out, and didn't realize it was getting dark. By the time I turned around, it was too late. It was pitch black. I couldn't see two feet in front of me." I shifted my weight slightly on the chair, and wouldn't you know it, the flashlight fell out of my pocket and onto the floor.

My dad stared at it. "You couldn't see, huh? So where'd that come from?"

I couldn't tell him where I had gotten it. That would ruin everything. "I saw it in the living room and grabbed it when I came in. I kept thinking how great it would have been to have had one of these tonight."

Aunt Gloria leaned over and picked up the flashlight. She examined it. "Not one of ours. Never seen it before."

Oh, thank you very much, Aunt Gloria. Way to be a real pal.

"That's about it. I got lost. It got dark. But I'm back now."

My dad folded his arms. The expression on his face indicated something bad was about to happen. I just knew it.

"So that's it, huh?" he said. "You got lost and it got dark? That's the best you can do?"

"Well…yeah. Don't you believe me?"

"Paulie, why do I feel you've left out certain parts of the story? There's got to be more to it."

"There isn't," I said.

"Okay, if that's the story you're sticking with, it's clear to me I can't trust you. So I need to treat you like a child." He paused. "For the remainder of this trip, you are grounded. You're not to leave this house under any circumstances. Do you understand?"

No! You can't do that to me. I have to see Guennie

again. I needed to do something. How could I make him trust me again?

"Dad, that's not necessary. I won't come back late anymore. I promise. You can't ground me."

"Oh, I can't? Oh, yes, I can. This conversation is over."

I looked at Uncle Buddy. I stared right at him. With my eyes, I pleaded with him to do something. I needed him to come to my defense. *Please, Uncle Buddy.* He knew about Guennie...well, sort of. He was my only hope.

"Peter?" he said.

"What is it?"

"I'm not telling you how to discipline your own son," Uncle Buddy said, "but don't you think you're being a little harsh?"

"From where I'm standing, Buddy, it does sound like you're trying to tell me how to handle this matter. No disrespect, but I'd prefer it if you would just butt out."

Uncle Buddy looked at me and shrugged.

I looked back and shook my head. I couldn't believe it. So that was it? That was his best shot? *Uncle Buddy, c'mon, fight for me.*

"Again, Peter, I'm not trying to step on your toes, but can I suggest an alternative?"

"No," my dad said.

"What is Paulie supposed to do?" Uncle Buddy said. "Watch TV and play shuffleboard all day? He'll go bananas."

"There are consequences for our actions," my dad said. "He'll just have to live with it. And considering how Mom's doing, we shouldn't be here that long."

Uncle Buddy stood up and walked over to where my dad was standing. "I'm going to throw something out. And hopefully you'll agree with me." He waited until my dad was looking right at him. "Let *me* be responsible for him. Wherever I go, he goes. That way you'll always know where he is and that he's safe. What do you say?"

"Do you know what you're asking?" my dad said. "It'll be like you have another appendage. You'll get tired of it pretty fast."

"And if I do, then he stays right here…under house arrest."

My dad rubbed his forehead.

"It'll give me a better chance to get to know my nephew. So are you okay with it?"

My dad sighed. He put his hand on the doorway to support himself. "Oh, all right."

I looked at Uncle Buddy and smiled. He had saved me. I was, however, hoping he didn't actually mean I had to stay with him all the time. He needed to let me see Guennie or he hadn't done anything to help me. I would have to work on him.

"I'm no parent," Aunt Gloria said, "but it seems to me the boy's getting off pretty easy."

For Christ's sake, why didn't she just keep her mouth shut. She was a miserable human being. And she might ruin everything.

"Lighten up, Gloria," Uncle Buddy said. He turned to me. "Hey, Paulie, how'd you like to spend the night at my place? It's not much. You'd have to sleep on the couch. But it'll allow you and your dad to have some space." He smiled.

I nodded.

"Why don't you run upstairs and put some things together," he said. "It's getting late."

I glanced at my dad.

"Well, go if you're going," he said.

I ran upstairs and threw a change of clothes in my duffle bag. I grabbed a toothbrush and deodorant. I was back downstairs in less than two minutes. I couldn't believe what Uncle Buddy had done for me. I'd owe him big-time for years to come.

Chapter 11

Uncle Buddy was waiting by the front door for me. I followed him out to the parking lot and jumped into his Corvair. He started it up and we climbed the hill.

"Thank you for what you did back there," I said. "You saved my life."

"You're welcome, but for my sake, we have to make this work. I know you want to see that girl again." He turned to me. "Did she have anything to do with why you were so late?"

I put my head down and refused to speak. I didn't want to have to tell anybody what had happened.

He tapped me on the shoulder. "You have to tell me the truth, or I'll turn around right here and take you back. Is that what you want?"

"No."

"Then tell me what happened."

I took a couple of deep breaths. "It did have something to do with her."

"Guennie?"

"Yeah. I just went over to her place..." I paused.

"To try to talk to her?"

I nodded.

"Paulie, I know what young love's all about. I teach high schoolers. I see it every day. And, believe it or not, I've been through it myself. There's nothing you can tell me I haven't already heard."

I was beginning to feel more comfortable. I had never before told an adult how I felt about girls. I'd had plenty of conversations with Mickey about them, but no one else.

"Well, when I got to her farm, she was the only one there. She was riding a horse. I thought it best to hide in the bushes. But she saw me. So we talked. And she told me to leave. Then we talked some more. And she told me to leave again."

"I'm seeing a pattern here," Uncle Buddy said. He was grinning.

"Then we heard the pickup truck coming. She didn't want me to be seen with her. She was afraid her brothers would...would react negatively."

"That's a nice way to put it."

"So we hid in the barn. Up in the loft. We talked some more. Then she left me alone until it was safe for me to leave. And that's why I was so late. If I had tried to get out of there earlier, I might have been seen, and that could have spelled disaster." I looked away. "Are you gonna tell my dad?"

Uncle Buddy smiled. "Are you kidding? This'll be our little secret."

"Thanks."

We drove in silence for the next couple of minutes. Then we pulled into the trailer park and up to Uncle Buddy's unit.

"Here we are," he said.

We got out and entered the trailer...er...mobile home. When I stepped in, I immediately saw a man sitting on the couch watching television.

"Oh," Uncle Buddy said. "Paulie, I'd like you to meet Jonathan. He's my roommate. Paulie's my nephew."

I extended my hand. "Hi," I said.

"Paulie's gonna stay with us for a couple of nights," Uncle Buddy said.

Jonathan smiled but it was what you might describe as a polite smile. I sensed he wasn't too keen on having me around. I started to wonder if this arrangement was a good idea or not.

"This couch opens up," Uncle Buddy said. "We've got plenty of room." He began removing cushions and piling them up on the floor. He lifted the bed up out from the couch. "Jonathan, would you mind getting me a couple of sheets from the linen closet?"

Jonathan made a face and disappeared. He returned moments later with a pair of yellow sheets and handed them to me. He then made a quick exit. Uncle Buddy was busily making the bed when he stopped and stared at me.

"We have to do something about your arms," he said. He dashed into the bathroom and came out with a tube of ointment. "Here," he said. "Rub this on that rash. It should help with the itching and the redness."

"Thanks," I said. "Hey, Uncle Buddy, I can finish up here."

"That's okay," he said. "I don't mind." He finished making up the bed, and then found an extra pillow in a nearby closet. "If you need anything, just yell. You can watch some TV if you want. You might be able to catch a little bit of the convention. It's an hour earlier there."

"What convention?" I said.

Uncle Buddy put his hands on his hips. "*What* convention? The Democratic National Convention. It's taking place right now. In your hometown. Chicago.

Paulie, you have to bone up on your current events."

I was embarrassed by the fact I hadn't picked up what he was referring to. I knew there was a political convention going on back home, but I never paid much attention to things like that. I didn't watch the ten o'clock news. I guess I wasn't very well informed. Another reason I wasn't college material.

"Oh, yeah, yeah," I said. "I knew it was going on. I just forgot."

Uncle Buddy sat down on the bed. He patted a spot next to where he was sitting for me to join him.

"What did we talk about in the car? You need to trust me. I want you to feel comfortable enough to tell me the truth. To tell me anything."

I stared at the floor.

"If you really didn't know the convention was going on, there's nothing wrong with admitting that."

I sighed. "I don't watch the news. I don't read the newspaper. I don't follow what's going on. I remember now that the convention is taking place. But I couldn't tell you who's there or what's going to happen."

Uncle Buddy just sat there for a minute and smiled. He seemed to be thinking about what he wanted to say.

He leaned over. "There is no knowledge that is not power." He stopped and stared.

It was as if he was waiting for me to comment on what he had just said. I wasn't sure what I was supposed to say. It was like he was quoting someone. *Quoting someone.* And then it hit me.

"Emerson?"

He nodded. "Ralph Waldo Emerson from 'Society and Solitude,' 1870." He put his hand on my shoulder. "Paulie, knowledge *is* power. You want to stand out at

118

school? With your circle of friends? With your co-workers? With the *ladies*?" He paused. "Make an effort to find out what's going on in the world. Watch the news. Read the newspaper. Take an interest in current events. Be a player, not a benchwarmer. Be someone people look to for advice. 'Gee, I wonder what Paulie would think about this,' they'll say." He stood up and then crouched down in front of me. "Emerson has all the answers. Think about it." He disappeared down the hallway.

I fell back onto the sofa bed and put my hands behind my head. I thought about the Emerson quotation: "There is no knowledge that is not power." Knowledge—something I had very little of. But it had been my choice. I chose to be uninformed. I chose to do the absolute minimum in classes. Studying didn't seem to have an upside for me.

I thought about Mickey and all the colleges he planned to apply to. It sounded kind of exciting. I didn't want to be missing out on all of that. I wondered what it would be like if I were to actually apply myself.

It was a little scary, though. What if I did try my hardest but still continued my downward spiral? Now that would be downright depressing. But in my heart, I knew if I had been a better student, I could have gotten better grades—grades good enough to get me into college. I had allowed myself to fall into the depths with all the other dregs of society. There was no pressure down there. You did just enough to get by. And what was the result? No knowledge. No power.

I closed my eyes and drifted off.

****

When I woke up, I wasn't sure where I was for a

minute. Then I remembered coming over to Uncle Buddy's. I also remembered the deal he had made with my dad—that he'd be my shadow. Wherever I went, he went. Or probably vice versa. If Uncle Buddy was around when I was trying to track down Guennie, it would definitely cramp my style. He knew what I was up to, but that didn't mean he'd have to follow me around like I was a baby. I would need to convince him, plead with him maybe, to allow me a little time off leash. I would need to assure him if he allowed me to be on my own for a little while each day, I wouldn't get into any trouble, and I'd obey all my curfews.

As I dug into my duffle bag for something to wear, the phone rang. It was sitting a few feet away on the coffee table. I was certainly the closest person to it, but I wasn't sure if I should answer it. After all, I was just a guest. It rang again and again. Finally Uncle Buddy emerged from the bedroom. He had on pajama bottoms but no shirt.

"You can get that if you want, Paulie."

"I didn't know if I should," I said.

Uncle Buddy reached over me and picked up the phone. "Hello." The expression on his face soon changed from tiredness to concern. "Okay, thanks for letting me know." He hung up the phone and sat on the end of the sleeper couch. "That was your dad. It seems your grandmother has taken a turn for the worse. He called the doctor. We'd better get over there."

Uncle Buddy made up a breakfast of scrambled eggs, hash browns, pork sausages, and English muffins. It looked and tasted better than anything you might find in a restaurant. Of course, I wasn't the best judge since we never, and I mean never, went out to eat. Not if my dad had anything to say about it.

"This breakfast is outstanding," I said.

"Why, thank you," he said. "I do pride myself on my cooking. I picked it up from my mother."

I decided to try and find out just how serious Uncle Buddy was about keeping an eye on me. I needed to casually work it into a conversation. I couldn't just blurt it out.

"So besides visiting Grandma, what else is on your agenda today?" I asked.

"Oh, I thought I'd spend some time at the library. I still have some lesson plans I need to finish up for the start of the school year."

"Boy, I didn't think teachers worked that hard."

Uncle Buddy chuckled. "You'd be surprised how busy a high school teacher can be. On most school nights, I'm usually up till eleven or twelve grading tests or papers. Don't judge how busy a teacher is by the time he or she spends in the classroom. There's plenty to keep us busy outside the classroom."

I sat back in my chair and smiled. "I'll remember that." Okay, enough of the small talk. It was time to find what really mattered. "So, while you're at the library, I was wondering where I'll be."

Uncle Buddy got up from the table and began clearing off the plates. "You'll be at the library...with me. That was the deal I made with your dad. I'm a man of my word." He placed the plates in the sink. "I'm sure you'll be able to find a good book to read. If you know what books you'll be reading in school this year, it'll be a good opportunity to get a head start on one of them." He ran water in the sink and added some dish soap. "If you thought, Paulie, I'd let you wander all over, well,

I'm afraid that can't happen. I'm responsible for you now. Sorry."

This was like being in prison—a fairly nice prison—but a prison nonetheless. If I wasn't able to be on my own for at least part of the time, I'd go nuts. I needed to see Guennie again. I needed to talk to her. I had to make Uncle Buddy see that. He seemed like a pretty reasonable guy. He would have to let me have some time alone. He would just have to.

"Uncle Buddy, can we have a man-to-man talk?"

He grinned and sat back down at the table. "Okay, what's on your mind?"

"I know you told my dad you'd keep an eye on me from now on, but I was just wondering if you'd see your way to give me just a little time alone. There are some things I have to do before we leave. And I need some space in order to do them. What do you say?"

He sat back in his chair and folded his arms. "So you want me to break the promise I made to your dad, is that it?"

Why did he have to put it like that? He made it sound so dishonest.

"What if I promised to stay out of trouble, and to be back on time? My dad wouldn't have to know anything about it. It would be our little secret." I waited for his response and hoped for the best.

He crossed his legs. "I'll tell you what. You stick close to me for the next couple of days and maybe, then maybe, I'll give you a little freedom. Can you do that?"

A couple of days? I didn't know if I had a couple of days. If Grandma died today or tomorrow, there wouldn't be any time to see Guennie. I needed to make him see that, but I needed to do so in a nice way—a way that made me seem cooperative. I would play along for today and hope he would lengthen the leash tomorrow.

"Okay, I think I can live with that."

"Good. So, let's get cleaned up and go over to the house. What do you say?"

I nodded. I dashed into the bathroom to wash up and brush my teeth. Then I put on my jeans and a clean T-shirt. While Uncle Buddy used the bathroom, I put the sleeper couch back together. Then I went into the kitchen and started washing the breakfast dishes. I would make it seem as though I was the perfect roomie. I wouldn't disagree or argue with anything he said. I would be a good soldier. And I would earn my leave.

Chapter 12

When we got to my grandparents' house, we found everyone upstairs in Grandma's bedroom—my dad, Aunt Gloria, Grandpa, and the doctor, who was listening to Grandma's heart.

"It's very weak," he said. He repositioned the instrument. "And I can hear a lot of fluid buildup in her lungs." He turned to face the group. "Very soon her organs will start shutting down. And then it's just a matter of hours." He reached into his bag, pulled out a bottle of pills, and handed them to my aunt. "If she regains consciousness, you can use these for the pain. But that's unlikely."

"How much time do you think we have?" my dad asked.

"It's impossible to say," the doctor replied. "Two to three days—tops." He stroked the top of her head. "She appears to be resting comfortably. Let's hope it's painless." He leaned in to Grandma. "You're a tough old gal, Sophia. You don't have to fight anymore. It's okay to let go." He straightened up, picked up his bag, and closed it. He looked at my aunt. "You won't need to call me again. There's nothing more I can do." He stood up and shook Uncle Buddy's hand, and then my dad's. He walked over to my grandfather and hugged him. "Hang in there, Paul." Grandpa was too choked up to reply. The doctor grabbed his fedora off the end of the bed and was just about to leave the room when he looked at my arms and stopped.

"Son, what is that?"

"Poison ivy, I think."

He dug into his bag and pulled out a tube of ointment. "Rub this on the affected areas three times a day. It'll help with the itching."

"Thank you," I said. I glanced at Uncle Buddy, who smiled and winked at me. Then I made the mistake of looking at my dad. He had this disgusted look on his face. He was probably thinking how dumb I was for having walked into a poison ivy bush in the first place. The doctor patted me on the shoulder and left.

"Looks like your trip to Leroy will be ending soon, Peter," Aunt Gloria said.

"I had a feeling it would be short," he said.

"I'm going to take Pop downstairs," Uncle Buddy said.

My dad turned to me. "Why don't you go with your grandfather."

I didn't say a word. I just followed orders. The last thing I wanted to do was set off my dad. Thanks to Uncle Buddy I had gotten a reprieve. I couldn't risk another grounding.

Uncle Buddy helped Grandpa down the stairs and set him up at the kitchen table.

"How about some coffee with anisette, Pop?"

"No," he said. "I think I want to go out to the back porch and sit on the swing. Mama and I used to sit there a lot."

"I can sit with him," I said.

My grandfather smiled, reached over, and grabbed the back of my neck. "That's good. That's good. Let me spend some time with my grandson. Once Mama's gone, I have a feeling you'll be headed back to Chicago. Right?"

"Probably," I said.

We walked out of the kitchen and through the dining room and living room before ending up on the back porch. We sat down and began to swing.

"I'm not sure I can go on without her," Grandpa said.

I wasn't sure if I was supposed to say something to make him feel better. Something like that is better handled by an adult. He just sat there in silence, so I decided to give it a shot.

"You're tough, Grandpa. You'll make out okay."

He put his arm around me. "I never had to deal with anything like this before," he said. Then he seemed to stop and think to himself. "Not since Dominick. I can still remember that day. Two army officers showed up at the front door. As soon as I saw them, I knew he was gone. Up until now that was the worst day of my life." He closed his eyes.

We continued to rock quietly. I wasn't sure if I should keep him talking or if he just needed some time to reflect on things. I decided on the former.

"Gramps, if you just give up, what'll happen to that magnificent garden of yours? The weeds'll grow and choke the plants to death. You can't let that happen. It's up to you to keep them alive."

He opened his eyes and smiled. "I know what you're trying to do, Paulie. And I appreciate it, but right now those plants don't seem quite as important."

"I'm not saying they're as important as Grandma or anything. I'm just saying that…" I wasn't really sure what I was saying. I was getting tied up in knots.

He patted my leg. "You're a good boy. Losing Mama will be a terrible thing, but because of it, I got back you and your dad. So don't worry, I'll be okay. I'll just need a little time to accept it."

We sat there for another half hour. We didn't converse. We just sat there. It seemed at times Gramps was in a trance of some kind. He would just stare into space. And then all of a sudden, he would return to reality and let out a long sigh.

The rest of the day was pretty quiet. There were a few neighbors who made their way up to Grandma's room to say goodbye. My dad spent the entire day up there. Uncle Buddy would go in and out periodically. Whenever I showed up at her room, my dad would shoo me away. Maybe I wanted to say goodbye too. Did he ever think of that? But I decided not to push it. It was a lose-lose proposition.

I found some lunchmeat in the fridge and made myself a sandwich for lunch. I sat around in the dance hall and played one-man shuffleboard until I got bored. Then I found a deck of cards and played solitaire for a while. I hadn't brought any reading material with me. I wasn't the kind of kid who carried a book around anyway. I knew some who did. I didn't care to be in their company. If you found me reading a book, it was because it was an assignment. I never picked up a book for pleasure. Although I had to say a few assigned books had kept me somewhat interested. But most I never bothered to read and simply relied on the Cliffs Notes®. I wasn't proud of myself, but I couldn't have been the only kid who did it.

By the time the clock hit three p.m., I was looking

for something—anything to keep me from going batty. What I really wanted to do was get out of this place and go look for Guennie. But I just didn't think it was a good strategy today. After what had happened last night, I needed to keep things low-key for a while.

I walked outside and looked around. I went to the back of the house. I wanted to see how steep that drop was down to the railroad tracks. When I worked up enough courage to look over the edge, I could just barely see the tracks. Weeds and grass had grown all around them. It was obvious they hadn't been in use for a while. When I strained to see what else was down there, I was able to see a bush with some red things all over it. Strawberries! It had to be. I remembered what my dad had said about how he and Uncle Dom used to pick strawberries down there and then play chicken whenever they heard a train coming. I wondered at that moment if I had the guts to go down there and pick a bowl of strawberries and give it to my dad as a peace offering.

And then, right on cue, I began scratching my arms. I had actually forgotten about the poison ivy for a while. That ointment was really working. I pulled the tube out of my pocket and applied it to the red areas on my arms again. I planned to put it on one more time when I went to bed. When I finished, I thought about those strawberries again. Should I do it? Should I try to safely climb down the side of this bank and go after my fortune? When I thought about the fact it was only the middle of the afternoon and I still had a lot more time to kill, I decided to do it. I went in the back door and into the kitchen. I found a cereal bowl in the pantry. This should do it, I thought.

I returned to the drop-off at the back of the house. I peeked over the edge. It was probably about twenty feet to the bottom. I would need to watch my footing. One misstep and I'd be in some deep shit. I walked up and down the edge hoping to find a spot that wasn't so steep. Finding none, I dropped onto my butt and slowly and steadily began my descent. As long as I was able to find a hole or an indentation in the side of the bank, I was okay. I was about a quarter of the way down when I got to thinking about how I was going to get back up the hill. I hadn't given that a lot of thought. I would hopefully find the same holes I was using on my way down to climb back up. At least, that was the plan.

I continued on down as carefully as possible. One slip and I would be headed for the steel beams of the Pennsylvania Railroad's former tracks. All the vegetation in the world wouldn't soften the blow. I was about halfway down the slope, still sliding on my butt, when a baby deer suddenly appeared at the bottom of the gulley. I stopped short. I knew deer were a lot more frightened of us than we were of them. I continued downward a couple feet, with each step getting ever so close to the deer and the bottom of the drop. When I was about ten feet from the bottom, my foot slipped and I ended up sliding all the way down on my butt, eventually hitting my knee on the railroad tracks. Oooh, that smarted. The cereal bowl went flying in the direction of the deer, who made a hasty exit.

I got up, rubbed my knee, retrieved the bowl, and headed to the strawberry bush. When I had a chance to examine it more closely, I realized the red berries I had seen earlier weren't strawberries at all. They were some kind of round red berries I had never seen before. I had no idea if they were safe to eat or not. Oh, great. I had just risked my life to pick a bowl of strawberries with the hopes of getting on my dad's good side, and it had turned out to be a wasted effort. I decided to scale the hill as quickly as possible and make it back up before anyone knew I had been down there.

As I attempted to climb back up, I was unable to find the holes I had used to navigate my way down. I kept looking for any ridge or rock I could use as a step. But every time I stepped on a rock, I would feel it give way, and soon I was back at the bottom sitting on my butt. This went on for twenty minutes or so. It didn't take me long to realize I wasn't going to be able to climb back up this hill without help. But help was the last thing I wanted. It would just be one more thing my dad would be pissed about. I hated to have to admit I had gotten myself into this pickle and needed someone's assistance. I made one last futile attempt to scale the hill, but it was no use. It was time to call for help.

"Can anybody hear me up there? It's me, Paulie. Help, anybody!" I continued to yell until I was hoarse. It was now late afternoon. No one was coming. My dad would probably be looking for me right about now. How had I managed to get myself into such a mess? About a half hour later, I thought I heard someone out on the back porch. "Help, anybody. I'm down here. Can anyone hear me?"

"Paulie?" a voice said. It was Aunt Gloria. She was standing at the top of the embankment with her arms crossed. "What the hell are you doing down there?"

"I was trying to pick some strawberries," I said.

"There haven't been strawberries down there in

years. What'd you do, get yourself stuck?"

"Kind of. I can't get back up."

She started to laugh. "Your old man has to see this." She started to walk away.

"No, please, Aunt Gloria, don't tell him."

She reappeared. She was scowling. "I'll be right back."

A few minutes later, she returned with a rope. She tied one end to a porch banister and threw the other end down the hill.

"All right, see if you can manage to get yourself up here now."

If it killed me, I would make it up there. I grabbed onto the rope and started to pull myself up. With each step, I could feel my hands slipping. At one point, I lost my footing and found myself dangling about ten feet from the bottom.

Aunt Gloria was now on her knees. She was holding onto the rope and was trying to pull me up. "You're too heavy," she said. "It won't budge."

I managed to find a rock with my foot to help get my bearings and restarted my ascent. I could feel the rope burns on my hands, but I would just have to ignore them. Then suddenly I could feel myself being pulled upward. When I looked, I could see my dad and Uncle Buddy had now joined the team. A couple of minutes later, I was up at the top and sitting on the edge with my legs dangling. I looked up at the others sheepishly.

"Do you mind telling me what you were doing down there?" my dad said. "Did you fall?"

"No, I went to pick some strawberries."

"Are there still strawberries down there?" my dad asked Aunt Gloria.

"Not for the last ten years or so."

My dad looked right at me. "Do you think maybe you should have asked someone before you decided to go down there?"

"I suppose so."

He shook his head. "Go get yourself cleaned up."

I needed to make him realize I wasn't just pulling some harebrained stunt but trying to do what he and his brother had done a million years ago.

"Dad, don't you remember how you told me about how you and Uncle Dominick would go down there and pick strawberries? And then you'd play chicken when you'd hear a train coming? I just wanted to surprise you with a bowlful of fresh strawberries. That's all."

"He just wanted to be like his dad," Uncle Buddy said. "You can't blame a kid for that, now, can you?"

My dad stared forward for what seemed like an eternity. "I still have to visit his grave."

I needed to get myself on the side of the good guys. "Well, what are you doing now?" I said. "Why don't we go do that while we're thinking about it?"

"Not now," my dad said. "It's still too soon." He climbed the stairs leading to the back porch and disappeared into the house.

"I thought it was a good idea," I said.

"Your dad and Dominick were very close," Uncle Buddy said. "He took Dom's death really hard."

"Don't you think it bothered me too?" Aunt Gloria said defensively. "Why Dominick decided to enlist, I'll never know. He threw his life away when he did that."

"I don't think those were his intentions," Uncle Buddy said. "He did what thousands of American boys did back then. They didn't think they were going to die.

They thought they were going to defend their country and then come back home and pick up right where they left off."

"Oh, what do you remember?" Aunt Gloria said. "You were just a kid."

"I remember it. But what I remember most is being thankful I was too young to fight. I'm not sure I would have enlisted if I'd been old enough." Uncle Buddy rubbed the top of my head. "I just pray you won't have to see military action."

I wasn't sure what Uncle Buddy had against the military. If I decided not to go to college, or if I flunked out, joining the army was an option I'd have to consider.

"I'm a pacifist," he said. "I don't believe in war. I wish I could make this Vietnam mess just go away. I still don't know why the heck we're over there."

"Pacifist?" Aunt Gloria said. "Shit. In my book, that's just another word for coward."

Uncle Buddy held out his hand to help me up. "C'mon, let's go. I've heard enough."

Chapter 13

For the remainder of the afternoon, things were quiet. There was little to no conversation among the siblings. It seemed Aunt Gloria's "coward" comment had left a bad taste in Uncle Buddy's mouth. He was ignoring her. I didn't care much for it myself. But I wasn't about to take on Aunt Gloria. You just couldn't win an argument with her. At four o'clock, Grandpa removed the Closed sign on the front door of the bar. Patrons strolled in and out for the next couple of hours. For the most part, it was a routine night. But it didn't stay that way.

Later in the evening, Uncle Buddy told Grandpa and my dad that he would close up and they should go to bed. No one had told me any differently, so I guessed I would be sleeping at Uncle Buddy's again that night. I spent most of the night watching TV and playing shuffleboard and solitaire. At about eleven, an old man in a straw hat came in. I immediately recognized him. He was Mr. Thompson, Guennie's dad. He sat down on one of the stools and demanded a beer. Uncle Buddy made eye contact with me. I think he was trying to alert me as to who this fellow was, but I already knew.

For the next hour, I had to listen to Mr. Thompson whine about the weather, the government, and just about anything else that came up for discussion. He was loud and argumentative. And he could curse with the best of them.

At a quarter to twelve, Uncle Buddy announced the bar would be closing in fifteen minutes and it was time for the last round.

"What are you talking about?" Thompson said. "I just got here."

"I'm just following county rules, sir," Uncle Buddy said. "Any establishment that serves alcohol has to close up at midnight. It's the law."

"Never heard of it."

"No disrespect, Mr. Thompson, but you've been here plenty of times. You know the rules."

"So how's about you make an exception for me," Thompson said.

Uncle Buddy shook his head. "Sorry, can't do it. They'll shut us down if they find out."

Mr. Thompson smiled. "Let me give you a little piece of advice. Don't you be trying to kick me out of here, friend."

"I'm afraid you'll have to leave at midnight."

Mr. Thompson just sat there and nursed his beer for the next ten or so minutes. The entire time, he stared daggers at Uncle Buddy. At midnight, the other patrons got up, tossed money on the counter, and left. All except Mr. Thompson.

Aunt Gloria walked into the bar and looked around. She turned to Uncle Buddy. "Time to close up, Buddy. What's the hold up?"

He pointed at Mr. Thompson and shrugged his shoulders.

She walked over to Thompson. "Hey, Travis, we gotta close up. It's time to go home."

He didn't budge.

Aunt Gloria folded her arms. "Buddy, throw him out."

Thompson began to laugh. "Throw me out? A little pipsqueak like him?"

Uncle Buddy reached over the counter and attempted to retrieve Thompson's empty beer glass. But Thompson was having none of it. He grabbed onto the handle and pulled it from Uncle Buddy's grasp.

"Get out!" Aunt Gloria yelled.

"I ain't ready to leave." He pushed his glass across the bar. "Fill 'er up," he said.

Uncle Buddy pointed to the clock. "How many times do I have to tell you—we can't serve alcohol after midnight."

"I don't see no clock, Tinkerbell," Thompson said.

Uncle Buddy pointed again to the one behind the bar. Mr. Thompson promptly picked up his beer mug and threw it at the clock, shattering the outside glass. Then he sat up, reached over the bar, grabbed another mug, and flung it against a large mirror. Pieces of glass flew all over. A large shard whisked by my head some twenty feet away. I wanted to help but I didn't know what to do.

"I don't have to take this crap from him," Aunt Gloria said. "I'm going to bed. Wake me when it's over." She turned and exited the bar.

Well, that was real nice. Nothing like abandoning your fellow man in his time of need. Uncle Buddy motioned for me to come over.

"There's a phone in the dining room," he whispered. "Dial the operator and ask her to connect you with the sheriff. Tell him what's going on here."

"Yeah, kid, go ahead and call the sheriff,"

Thompson said. "He's a buddy o' mine. He won't do anything."

I ran out of the bar, through the kitchen, and into the dining room. I picked up the phone and dialed zero.

"Operator. Can I help you?" a voice said.

"Can you connect me with the sheriff, please," I said.

"One moment."

And then a few seconds later. "Sheriff's office."

"Hello, my name is Paulie Passero. I'm at the Happy Time Lounge in Leroy. There's a rowdy man in the bar throwing things and breaking mirrors and…"

"You don't sound old enough to be a bar patron, son," the man said.

"I'm not. Paul Passero is my grandfather. He's asleep. My Uncle Buddy is trying to close up the bar, but this man won't let him."

There was a pause at the other end. "Okay, I'll be there in a few minutes."

"Thanks." I hung up. I went back into the bar to make sure Uncle Buddy was okay. Thompson was now behind the bar smashing every glass he could get his hands on. I felt helpless. Then I got an idea. I ran upstairs to wake my dad. He would want to know about this. I went into our bedroom and nudged him.

"Dad, wake up."

"What? What's going on?"

"There's a guy in the bar breaking everything— mirrors, glasses, everything."

"There's what?"

He jumped out of bed, threw his pants on, and ran downstairs. When we entered the bar, Thompson had Uncle Buddy cornered. He was holding an empty beer bottle and was swinging it. My dad ran back behind the bar and threw his arms around Thompson.

"Drop it, pal," my dad said.

But Thompson then went after him. He broke my dad's hold and swung the bottle at him.

"You wanna play too?" Thompson said.

My dad was in his bare feet. He was stepping on broken glass. My heart was racing.

Then the front door swung open and a voice rang out. "Thompson! Put it down! Now!" It was the sheriff.

Thompson dropped the bottle and put his hands up. "We were just having a little fun here, Fred. There was no need to bother you."

The sheriff looked around the bar at all the broken glass. "You're coming with me tonight."

"No, just let me go home. I'll be good. I promise."

The sheriff worked his way behind the bar and up to his prisoner. "Hands behind your back." He pulled a set of handcuffs from his belt and secured Thompson. "Buddy, I assume you want to press charges."

"Absolutely."

"Why don't you stop by the office sometime tomorrow to fill out the paperwork."

"Okay."

The sheriff turned toward my dad. "It's nice to see you, Peter. It's been a while."

"It has been, Fred. How are you?"

"I could use fewer nights like these," he said, "but for the most part, I can't complain. You take care." He escorted his prisoner out of the bar.

Uncle Buddy walked to the front door, put the Closed sign back up, and locked it. "I think we'll be closed for a couple of days, until we get this mess cleaned up."

"Just leave it for now," my dad said. "You and Paulie should go get some sleep."

"You know, Peter, I worry about Pop being here alone when something like this happens."

"I know what you mean. It concerns me too."

"You don't know how many times I've tried to talk him into retiring," Uncle Buddy said. "But he won't listen."

"Maybe if we team up we can talk some sense into him," my dad said.

"I doubt if it'll do any good, but we can try." He flipped off the lights. "C'mon, Paulie, let's hit the sack."

****

I awoke the next morning with the intention of finagling a little *me time* today. I had gone an entire day without seeing Guennie. I was having withdrawal symptoms. I needed a fix badly. I had to convince Uncle Buddy he could trust me to be on my own for a while. After what had happened at the bar last night, I was hoping he would have more faith in me. When he needed me to contact the police, I had done so calmly and efficiently. I would think that might count for something.

I got dressed and cleaned up before he or Jonathan awoke. I thought about trying to make breakfast for all of us, but I wasn't really too handy in the kitchen. Over the years, my mom had spoiled me. I never really had to fend for myself when it came to preparing meals. Uncle Buddy found me with my nose in the refrigerator when he got up.

"What are you looking for?" he asked.

"I thought I'd make breakfast for all of us, but I don't know where to start."

"Get away from there," he said. "That's my job." He pointed to the table. "Sit down. What would you like?"

"Cereal's fine."

"I think we can do better than that. How about waffles?"

"Sounds great," I said.

I watched as Uncle Buddy added the ingredients into a bowl, mixed the batter, and spooned it out onto a hot iron. The waffles, dare I say, were picture perfect. This man really knew what he was doing in the kitchen. I guess if you never marry, you need to learn how to do things for yourself. Uncle Buddy would be a great catch for some lucky lady someday. I wondered why he had never married. I guessed when you grew up in a really small town, the pickin's were pretty slim. I was sure he'd find love someday.

Speaking of love, this might be a good time for me to wear down Uncle Buddy. I needed to hunt down Guennie today, and I couldn't do that with a babysitter.

"So what's on the agenda today?" I said.

Uncle Buddy sat back in his chair. "What would you like to do?"

Now how should I answer that question? I knew exactly what I wanted to do today, but I wasn't so sure if I should share that.

"Nothing special," I said.

"About twenty miles from here, there's a railroad museum," he said. "That might be fun."

Oh, God. That was the last thing I wanted to do. Walking around all day and looking at old locomotives and coal cars and cabooses—if that was even a word—was not my idea of fun.

"I was hoping to stay close to home today," I said. "You know, in case anything happens with Grandma." I was hoping he would buy that.

"You're absolutely right. We should stay close to home." He pointed at me. "Now you're thinking."

I added butter and syrup to the waffles and cut them up. I ate and smiled occasionally. I had to get to the point. No more beating around the bush. I needed him to let me solo today.

"Uncle Buddy?"

"Yeah."

The bedroom door opened and Jonathan appeared. He was in his underwear—a T-shirt and briefs.

"Oops, sorry, guys," he said. He retreated to the bedroom and came back out in pajama bottoms.

"What is it?" Uncle Buddy said.

"I'm not sure how to put this."

"Let me guess," he said. "You'd like to be on your own today. Is that it?"

I nodded enthusiastically. "It won't be all day. And I'll be back whenever you say. I promise."

He sighed. "Paulie, you have to be back when I ask you to, and you have to come back in one piece. Can you do that?"

"Absolutely." I jammed the remainder of the waffle into my mouth. I almost choked trying to get it down. I took my plate and glass to the sink and rinsed them out. "Okay, so when do I have to be back?"

"Five o'clock?"

That was outstanding. "Perfect," I said. "I really appreciate this, Uncle Buddy."

I turned and headed to the door.

"Paulie?"

"Yeah?"

"While you're out, do you mind stopping by the post office and picking up the mail for me and Grandpa?"

"Sure."

"And one more thing. I have a feeling I know where you're headed. Please be careful. Those boys are bad news. Don't get hurt out there."

Uncle Buddy was so cool. I nodded, smiled, and left the trailer. I decided to head to the post office first. Might as well get that out of the way. As I made my way down the various streets, I took note of some of the businesses I passed. I could use them as landmarks if I ever got lost. At one point, I came upon the sheriff's office. Well, it was good to know where that was. I was only about a block from the post office when a green pickup came roaring down the street. Country music was blasting from the cab. And then I realized it was the Thompson truck. There were three people sitting in the back—two boys and Guennie. I quickly ducked behind a newspaper stand and watched the truck slow down and stop right in front of the post office.

Guennie jumped out and went in. As badly as I wanted to see her today, I just didn't have the guts to walk right past her brothers and enter the post office. A minute or so later, she came out with a handful of mail. She walked around the truck and handed it to the driver, who appeared to be one of her brothers.

And then I remembered. Her dad must still be in jail. I wondered if they would stop by the sheriff's office and pick him up on their way back. Guennie then reached into the back and grabbed what looked like a towel. She stepped back from the truck as it peeled off leaving her standing alone in front of the post office. I wasn't sure what was happening, but I decided not to show myself until I knew it was safe.

She started walking north. At least I thought it was north. I didn't have my bearings in this town. I looked for the sun. It was on my right. Okay, then it *was* north. I followed her down one street, then another, then another. I kept far enough back so she wouldn't notice me. Soon we were out of the downtown area and in an open field. It was getting a little harder to stay undetected. I crouched down in the tall grasses. She never once looked back to see if anyone was behind her. She was a pretty cool customer. I could see railroad tracks in the distance. They were on a hill, elevated about eight to ten feet. And there was a freight train that had come to a stop on the tracks. Guennie was headed right for it.

I stayed about seventy-five yards behind her at all times. At that distance, even if she did turn around, it would be difficult for her to determine who was trailing her. She was headed straight for the train. I wasn't sure what she was up to. Was she going to wait for it to move? Maybe it did this every day and she knew when it would start back up. But the train wasn't budging. When she got closer to it, she scaled the hill and got up right next to it. Then I saw her bend down...and she disappeared.

What had just happened? She hadn't gotten on the train. Where was she? I broke into a jog and followed her exact path. When I got up to the hill, I realized what she had done. As crazy as it sounded, she had crawled under one of the boxcars to get to the other side. Was she nuts? Didn't she know how dangerous that was? What if the train suddenly began to move? It would jolt forward. And anybody or anything under it was a goner.

I climbed the hill and got up right next to the train. I bent down to see if I could tell what was on the other side. But it was impossible to see anything. I had to make a decision.

Was this girl worth risking my life for? Or had I been fooling myself all along that someone like me could ever end up with someone like her? If I had been, then there was no way I was going to risk life or limb with this stunt. I thought about it for a minute. If I waited much longer, it was doubtful I'd be able to follow her. She would be so far ahead of me I wouldn't know where she was. It was do or die. And this wasn't just a figure of speech. The *die* part could actually happen.

Part of me wanted to abandon this quest. This girl hadn't shown one iota of interest in me. Not to mention the physical danger of getting caught by her brothers. There was a clear downside here. Then there was that face, and that figure, and that hair, and that soft skin...and the fact this was the first girl I had ever been able to talk to. There was just something about her that fascinated me. It was hard to explain.

I got down on all fours, took a deep breath, gritted my teeth, and shuffled under the boxcar. I had made it to the other side and the train hadn't moved. I was safe. Until, of course, I had to crawl back under it to get home. I couldn't think about that now.

When I looked out, I saw Guennie. She was

swimming. On the other side of the train was a swimming hole. It didn't look completely natural. I was guessing it was manmade. Now I knew what the towel was for. I didn't think she had seen me yet. I climbed down the hill and walked up to the water's edge. On the shore were her towel, her blouse, and her jean shorts. She was up to her neck in the water.

"Oh, great," she cried. "What are you doing here?"

"I...I came for a swim."

She rolled her eyes. "I can't seem to get rid of you."

I wasn't sure how to respond. "So how's the water?" Now that was a stupid thing to say. I needed to do better than that.

"It's fine for me," she said, "but you're not welcome here. This swimming hole is only for locals. No tourists allowed."

I plopped down on the ground. "Okay, I'll just sit here on the shore then."

She shook her head. "Why are you following me?"

I knew damn well why I was following her, but how could I explain it to her without it sounding corny?

"I just...I just like being around you. That's all."

"It's not safe for you to be here. My brothers'll be back to pick me up soon. Trust me, you don't want to be here when they come."

I wanted to sound fearless. I grinned. "I'll take my chances."

"You can't say I didn't warn you."

Okay, it was time for a nice, normal conversation. What I needed was a clever opener.

"So how come your parents named you Guinevere?"

"You don't want to know."

"I do. Really."

She sighed. "All right, stand up and turn around."

"What? I don't understand."

"I only have my underwear on. And you're not about to see me like that."

"You're not wearing a bathing suit?"

"I would love to—but bathing suits cost money. Now will you please just turn your back."

I stood up and faced the train.

"Don't you dare turn around until I tell you to," she said. "Do you understand?"

"I promise I won't look."

"You'd better not."

I really wanted to look, but I had given her my word. It wouldn't be right to have lied to her. But I would have killed to have seen Guennie in her underwear. I could hear the splashing of the water as she walked out of the swimming hole. I could hear some grunting as she got dressed.

"All right, you can turn around now."

I spun around and knew instantly I was in love. Water dripped from her hair as she toweled it off. She stood on the shore barefoot and in cutoffs. Her legs were long and tanned. She tied the ends of her blouse around her waist, making her navel visible.

She was gorgeous. I had never been around a girl this beautiful before. I couldn't believe I was having a conversation with her. I would never have been able to do this back home. I couldn't wait to tell Mickey about Guennie. Although he probably would never believe me.

She walked a little closer to me and sat down on

the ground. I took her cue and joined her. The shore was a mixture of dirt and sand, but I didn't care.

"So what did you want to know?" she asked.

"Why your parents named you Guinevere."

She smiled. It was the first time I had seen her smile. And, boy, did she have a great smile.

"It was my mom's idea. She was a big fan of the knights of the round table. You know, King Arthur stories? She used to read them to me when I was little. Guinevere was his queen. She always loved that name. Me too." She looked out over the water wistfully. She was still smiling. I could tell she missed those days.

"So she doesn't read you those stories anymore?"

Her smile faded. "No, no more." She turned and looked at me. "My mom died when I was eleven."

"I'm sorry." I wasn't sure what else to say, but I needed to keep her talking. I wanted to know everything about her. "Did your dad read those stories then?"

She laughed. "Yeah, right. Ahh…no. I'm not sure if he knows how to read. I've never seen him pick up a book," she said disgustedly. She stared forward for a moment. "But I still read those books at bedtime. I think my mom would have liked that."

What to say next? What to say next? And then I had something. "Oh, I'm sorry about your dad."

"What about him?"

"We had to call the sheriff last night. He was tearing up my grandfather's bar. I guess he spent the night in jail."

"Don't worry about it," she said. "You did me a favor. It was the first good night's sleep I've had in months. Nobody to bother me." Her expression suddenly changed. It was as if she had said something I wasn't supposed to hear.

"What do you mean?"

"Nothing." She stood up. "Listen, you'd better get out of here. My brothers'll be here any minute."

I knew I should take her advice, but we were having this really nice conversation and I didn't want it to end.

"When are you going home anyway?" she said.

"In a few days, I guess. I have to be back before school starts. Although I wouldn't mind missing a few days."

"You don't know how lucky you are," she said. "If I had a chance to go to school, I'd never miss a day."

"You like school?" I said.

"I did. School was my only chance to get out of this place. Get a high school degree. Go to college. And get out of Leroy. That was my plan...until my dad yanked me out."

"You wanted to go to college?"

"Hell, yes."

"Do you ever worry you won't be able to cut it in college?"

She smiled. "Just give me the chance. I'll make it if it kills me."

"I'm just not sure I'm cut out for it," I said.

"Will your parents let you go if you want to?" she asked.

"Why sure. I think they want me to go."

She shook her head. "What exactly is wrong with you? You have the chance to go to college, and you *don't* want to go? Well, let me tell you—if I had the chance, nothing, and I mean nothing, would stop me."

"It's just that…"

"I already know what I'd do," she said. "I'd major in English. I'd become a famous author, and I'd live in New York. No, wait a minute. That's not far enough away from Leroy. Make that Los Angeles."

I smiled. She seemed to have her future all planned out, but based on her current situation, it appeared doubtful if any of it would happen.

"Going to college is the only way out of this town," she said. I'm not gonna be like all the other girls around here. They go to high school, unless they've gotten themselves knocked up, that is. Then they get married to a guy who works at the brickyard, and they get fat and become baby machines. That's not gonna happen to me."

The sound of an engine could be heard on the other side of the tracks.

"Oh, shit. That's gotta be my brothers. You have to get out of here."

"I need to see you again."

"Listen, Paulie, you're a nice guy, but this is never gonna work. You're leaving in a few days. And even if you lived here, it wouldn't work. Bad things happen to people who show any interest in me. Just go home and forget you ever met me."

"Hey, Guennie," a voice yelled out.

"I'll be there in a second."

"I'm coming over," the voice said.

"Oh, great," she said. "He'll see you. You have to hide." She looked around for something that might give me cover. "The water! Get in the water! Go under and hold your breath."

I froze.

"Now!" she screamed.

I ran into the water with my clothes on, with my shoes on, with everything on. I got up to my waist and looked back. She motioned for me to go underwater. I took one large breath and dropped down.

Chapter 14

I started counting. I held my breath as long as I could. When I got to thirty, I couldn't hold it any longer. My head popped out of the water. I rubbed my eyes and snuck a peek. I could just see one of Guennie's brothers crawling back under the railroad car. She must have already gone under. As I walked to the shore, I heard an engine roar from the other side of the train. They were gone. It was now safe.

I sat down on the ground and assessed the damages. Everything on me was completely soaked. How would I explain this? The sun was out. I couldn't claim I got caught in a downpour. I couldn't say I decided to go swimming, because who goes swimming with their clothes on? I might actually have to tell the truth for once. I got up, scaled the hill, crossed my fingers with the hopes the train wouldn't move, and successfully shuffled under the boxcar. I was hoping that was the last time I would be taking my life in my own hands.

I decided to go back to Uncle Buddy's and dry off. I was hoping no one would be at his trailer so I could change. I had some dirty clothes from the day before that would have to do. Halfway there, I remembered I was supposed to pick up the mail. I made a detour and walked back into town in the direction of the post office. With each step I took, my gym shoes squeaked. I must have looked pretty silly walking down the street soaking wet from head to toe. Most of the people I passed on the sidewalk stared at me. Some smiled. Others laughed to themselves, but no one said a word.

As I passed the sheriff's office, I stopped in my tracks when I saw a green pickup truck parked around the corner. I ducked back behind the edge of the building so I couldn't be seen. Guennie and two of her brothers sat in the back of the truck. I decided it was probably best if I crossed the street and kept my distance from the Thompsons. But before I could make my escape, Mr. Thompson and one of his sons emerged from the sheriff's office. I tried to avoid eye contact, but it was too late.

"Hey, you, kid," Thompson yelled out.

I turned momentarily, and then continued on my way across the street.

"That's the kid who called the cops on me last night. I'm sure of it." He slapped his son on the shoulder. "Get him," Thompson said.

I kept walking. By the time I got to the other side of the street, the oldest Thompson brother had caught up to me. He was standing in front of me with his arms folded, blocking my path.

"Where you going?" he said.

I ignored him and attempted to walk around him. I felt a tug on the back of my shirt.

"You ain't goin' nowhere," he said.

I tried to pull away but soon found myself in a headlock. "I got him, Pa."

The elder Thompson walked up to us. "Because of you, kid, I spent last night in a smelly jail. That wasn't very nice, now, was it?" He was poking his finger in my chest. By this time, the other boys had joined us.

The grip around my neck was so tight I was having a hard time breathing.

"I know that kid from somewhere," one of the boys said.

"He's one of them damn Passeros," Mr. Thompson said. "And somebody's gotta teach him a lesson."

"Let me do it, Pa," the oldest boy said. The other boys started laughing.

"Let him go," a voice said. It was Guennie. She was running up to where we were standing.

"This has nothing to do with you, girl," her father said.

"You deserved what you got last night, Pa," she said.

"Why, you little bitch," he said as he raised his hand to slap her. But before he could connect, a large hand reached in and grabbed hold of Thompson's arm. It was the sheriff.

"Whatever you do to these kids in your own home is your business," the sheriff said. "But you won't be doing it on my streets. You understand?"

Thompson lowered his arm. "Sure, Fred, whatever you say."

The sheriff glanced at the brother restraining me. "Let him go."

The oldest brother released his grip. I rubbed my neck and took a few deep breaths.

"Now, all of you, on your way...now," the sheriff said.

Mr. Thompson held up his hands as if he were surrendering. "You won't have a problem with us." He waved at his sons. "Let's go." He grabbed Guennie by the back of her blouse. "You got a fresh mouth, girl. You'll get yours when we get home. Get in."

The sheriff waited until the Thompsons were a few feet away. "Once we figure out the damages from last night, you'll have thirty days to pay 'em...or you'll be back in jail. Understand?"

Mr. Thompson locked his jaw. He didn't appear happy with the news, but he didn't say a word. The sheriff stood next to me until the Thompsons drove off. I watched him as his eyes examined me from head to toe. He removed his hat and scratched the top of his head.

"What happened to you, boy?"

"It's a long story."

"And I don't have the time to listen." He turned and headed back to his office. When he was about halfway, he stopped short. "You better stay away from those boys. I'm not gonna be around every time they try to rearrange your face."

"I'll be careful. And thanks a lot, Sheriff."

He nodded and was on his way.

I could tell by the sun it was about noon. Uncle Buddy was probably wondering what I was up to today. I continued my trek to the post office. The entire time I couldn't get one particular image out of my head—the one where Guennie's father raised his hand to strike her. He was big and strong. She was small and frail. He could do some real damage. And was it my fault? If I hadn't called the police the night before, then this ugly scene would never have happened. If he did lay a hand on her when they got home, and he probably would, it'd be on me. But what was I supposed to do? Uncle Buddy needed someone to call the authorities to stop

Thompson from completely destroying the bar. What choice did I have, really? I never thought my actions might end up hurting Guennie. I felt bad—really bad. I needed to see her again. I needed to find out if she was okay.

When I got to the post office, I found Norman behind the main window.

"How yah doing, Paulie. Let me get the mail for you." He disappeared momentarily. When he returned, he was holding a stack in his hand. "Do you want Buddy's too?" he said.

"Yeah, that would be great. Thanks."

He vanished once again and came back with a smaller batch of mail. "Here you go." As he was handing me the letters, he seemed to be studying me. "Can I ask you a question?"

"Sure."

"How did you manage to get yourself so wet?"

It was a legitimate question. I needed to be up front with Norman. He had saved my neck earlier.

"Well, to be perfectly honest, I was over at the swimming hole and I needed a place to hide since Guennie's brothers showed up."

"So you hid underwater?"

I shrugged. "It was the only thing I could think of. Actually, I should give the credit to Guennie. She's the one who thought it up."

"She's a smart girl." He smiled. "What did I tell you earlier about her brothers? They do crazy stuff. You gotta be careful."

"I will. Thanks." I left the post office and headed for Uncle Buddy's. I was hoping the sun would dry me off before I got there, but that wasn't the case. The minute I opened the door, Uncle Buddy did a double take. He put down the book he was reading.

"What happened to you? And can you tell me why you're soaking wet?"

"Do I have to?"

"I think it would be nice," he said with a half smile.

I told him about seeing Guennie and following her to the swimming hole. I left out the part where I snuck under a train. I told him how I had to hide underwater from her brothers. I was going to stop there, but I felt I owed him the complete story. I told him about the little dust-up in town outside the sheriff's office. He sat there and let me finish before saying a word.

"Paulie, can you stay close to home for the rest of the day? Can you do that for me? I promised your dad I'd keep you in one piece. Every time you go out, you seem to get into some kind of trouble."

"I don't mean to. It just sort of follows me."

"Why don't you sit tight for a little while." He got up off the couch. "Come with me." I followed him down a hallway to a small alcove with a built-in bookcase. It was completely full.

"Wow," I said. "How many books are in there?"

"Hundreds, probably. And if I lived in a real house, and not this mobile home, I'd have a lot more. Every year I have to give some away just to make room for the new ones."

"You must be a big reader," I said.

"I suppose it has more to do with the fact I'm an English teacher. I have to read all the books before I assign them," he said. "Well, listen, the reason I brought you over here is because we need to find something to keep you busy. You can't be chasing a girl around all day. If we can get you interested in a good book, then maybe you wouldn't be so restless. What do you say? Are you game?"

"Sure," I said. But I didn't mean it. In my entire life, I couldn't ever remember just picking up a book to read just for the heck of it. I just wasn't the best of readers. But Uncle Buddy had been really good to me on this trip. I wanted to make him happy, so I needed to seem enthusiastic about his suggestion. "I have to admit I'm not a very good reader. I probably haven't read any of these books. Is there one you'd recommend?"

"Hmm, let me see." He began running his finger over the spine of each book when he suddenly stopped. "How about this one?" He handed it to me.

"*Lost Horizon*?" I said.

He nodded.

"By James Hilton. So what's it about?"

He smiled and tilted his head back and forth. "Oh, Paulie, I don't want to give it away. Let's just say it's about a magical world in the Far East. And it's about a man whose life is forever changed when he finds it."

I flipped the book over, opened the back cover, and went to the last page.

"What are you doing?" he said.

I shook my head. "Two hundred and seventy-two pages. I'll need a month to finish it."

Uncle Buddy laughed. "Be serious."

"I am. It'll take me forever to get through this."

"Here's what I want you to do. Go into the kitchen. Sit down. And start this book. I'll bet you get hooked in no time. Heck, you might even finish it today."

"Finish a book in one day? I don't think so. I'm a really slow reader." Who was he kidding? There was no way that was going to happen.

"I've done it dozens of times." He tapped on the book's cover. "This isn't the easiest book in the world to read. It will challenge you. But I think that's what you need right now." He put his hand on my shoulder. "I have a feeling you've taken some shortcuts with your education in the past. Am I right?"

I nodded. I was finally being honest with someone about my ineptitude in the classroom. This was one of the first times I could remember I was admitting my shortcomings. With my parents, I was pretty much noncommittal. I didn't say much. I didn't come up with excuses. I just handed them my report card. They'd make faces, and I'd go up to my room. But somehow I was able to open up to Uncle Buddy. I wasn't sure why. Maybe it was because he wasn't judgmental. He didn't nag me; instead he encouraged me.

"Think of this trip to Leroy as an awakening for you. When you head back to Chicago, return as a new person. More worldly. More confident. More hungry to learn. It'll be just what you need if you plan to go to college." He smiled. "Go dry off, get changed, and enter the world of *Lost Horizon*. After all, 'The reader and the book, either without the other is naught.'"

"Don't tell me. Emerson? Right?"

"From 'Society and Solitude'—1870. Emerson believed a reader without a book is incomplete. You should always be reading a book." He winked. "Now get to work. I have to run over to the sheriff's office to sign a complaint against Mr. Thompson."

So I got to work. Maybe Uncle Buddy was right. Maybe I needed to get my mind off Guennie. Lately I was obsessed with her. But I couldn't stop thinking about her father almost hitting her. I wondered if he had done so when they got back to the farm. I was worried about her. It was hard to get her out of my head. But I needed to try. I took my duffle bag and went into the bathroom. I stripped down to my birthday suit and threw on the clothes I had worn yesterday. They didn't smell too great but at least they were dry. Then I emerged and headed into the kitchen. I took a deep breath and dove in.

Page one. Prologue. *Cigars had burned low, and we were beginning to sample the disillusionment that usually afflicts old school friends who have met again as men and found themselves with less in common than they had believed they had.* I looked at the clock. Noon. I would try to read for half an hour...if it didn't kill me first.

An hour later, I raised my head.

"Do you want some lunch?" Uncle Buddy said as he walked in from outside.

"No, that's okay. I'm not hungry yet. Thanks anyway." I jumped back in, and I didn't come up until about 4:30. I had become so engrossed in this novel that I lost all track of time. I had read chapter after chapter until I reached the end. I couldn't believe it. I had actually done it. I had read a book in one sitting.

Who would have believed it? I had to admit it had been a little difficult to get into at first, but soon I was hooked. Uncle Buddy was right. I had immersed myself in the land of Shangri-La, a Utopian society in the Himalayas of Tibet. I imagined myself as Hugh Conway, a member of the British diplomatic service, who finds inner peace and love in a strange land, only to lose it all.

But the story doesn't end there. I'd rather not give it away. You'll have to find out for yourself.

Chapter 15

When I informed Uncle Buddy I had finished the book, he hugged me and laughed. He was so supportive. He knew all the right things to say to a kid. I'll bet he would have made a great father. I could just see him chasing around little ones, and inspiring older ones. He would have loved it. And they would have loved it as well.

Uncle Buddy grilled some burgers for dinner. They were delicious. Let me tell you, he was one solid cook. We sat at the kitchen table and talked for hours. We discussed high school, college, my parents, Aunt Gloria, my grandparents, and much more. He was so easy to talk to. I was starting to get depressed that when Grandma passed on, we'd be headed home, and Uncle Buddy would still be here. I sure was gonna miss him.

At 8:30, he suggested we go over to the Happy Time Lounge and look in on the others. I knew he wanted to see how his mother was doing. We hopped in his Corvair and headed to the other side of town.

When we got there, we found my dad and Grandpa behind the bar still cleaning things up. They had decided to close the bar for a few days to get things in order. I went into the dance hall and flipped on the TV. I needed to find a program that would hold my interest until bedtime.

But every channel I went to was covering the

Democratic National Convention in Chicago. Boring politicians. Boring speakers. Boring reporters. It was brutal. Then the news anchor talked about something going on outside the convention. Thousands of anti-war protestors had assembled in nearby Grant Park. Most appeared to be supporters of Eugene McCarthy. When one of them took down an American flag, riot police moved in. They began beating the demonstrators with nightsticks. The police were pelted with rocks and bottles and concrete. It was chaotic.

"What are you watching?" Uncle Buddy said.

"There's a bunch of riots outside the hotel where the convention's going on."

Uncle Buddy turned up the sound on the TV. "Oh, my God!" he said. "What are they doing to those kids?" Chants of "Hell, no, we won't go" could be heard from the demonstrators. "Look at how they're manhandling those reporters," he said. "You're watching history, Paulie."

I wasn't sure whose side to take—the protestors who were throwing things at the police, or the police who were responding with nightsticks and clubs. One thing was sure—I was glad I was here and not back home tonight.

"This is going to be a black eye for the city of Chicago *and* the Democratic Party," he said. "These images will forever haunt Humphrey or McCarthy or whoever ends up with the nomination."

Uncle Buddy was right. Hubert Humphrey won the nomination only to be soundly defeated by Richard Nixon in November. Voters apparently remembered the chaos they saw at the convention and they associated it with the Democratic Party.

As I watched the coverage both inside and out, I wondered what it would be like to be a news reporter covering the convention. An hour ago, I'd found all of this deathly boring, but now it was kind of interesting. These reporters were serving a purpose. They were sharing breaking news with the rest of America. I wondered how difficult it might be to do something like that. I was guessing I could start at the newspaper at school and see how I liked it. And then if I did, I could probably major in journalism in college...if I got in, that was. I had two years to turn things around.

I wondered if I could do it. I knew if Uncle Buddy were a teacher at my high school, then I was sure I could right my wrongs academically. But he wouldn't be there to support me and inspire me. I wasn't sure if I had what it took to make this conversion alone. I knew in my heart I was capable of doing better. I just needed to get off my butt and put in an honest day's work. The more I thought about it, the more I could see myself as a successful network journalist reporting the news to the nation.

While I was watching the convention coverage, I hadn't noticed Mr. Thompson enter the bar. He was talking to my dad and Uncle Buddy. They all had pretty serious looks on their faces. I wanted to find out what I was missing, so I casually positioned myself close enough to hear their conversation.

"So that's how it's gonna be," Thompson said. "Whether you like it or not."

"Let me get this straight," Uncle Buddy said. "You want us to drop the charges *and* pay for the cleanup ourselves? You've got to be kidding."

"I'm not kidding," Thompson said. "I'm dead

serious."

"I think my brother and I are in complete agreement," my dad said. "We're not interested in your offer."

Thompson took his straw hat off and slapped it against his thigh. "It ain't an offer. It's what's gonna happen...unless, of course, you want to take your chances."

"What's that supposed to mean?" Uncle Buddy said.

"Well, I'll just tell you." He pointed to the broken mirrors. "That ain't nothing compared to the kind of shit you're in for if you don't drop this whole thing."

The door opened and one of the Thompson boys stuck his head in. "Are you coming, Pa?"

Thompson spun around. "You get the hell out of here unless you want the same thing your sister got."

My heart began to race. He *had* done something to Guennie. But what exactly?

"You been warned," Thompson said, and he turned to leave. He exited the bar and slammed the door behind him. I ran over to the window and watched him jump back into his pickup and storm off in the opposite direction of his farm. The three Thompson boys were in the back but there was no sign of Guennie.

"Should we call the sheriff?" my dad asked.

"We have to," Uncle Buddy said. "That was a threat."

I knew exactly what I had to do. It wouldn't be pleasant if I got caught, but I just had to. I ran over to Uncle Buddy and whispered to him.

"I gotta check on something. Please cover for me. I'll be back in a little bit." I didn't wait for his response.

I ran upstairs and into our bedroom. I grabbed the car keys off the dresser and ran down the stairs and out the back door. I had never taken the car before without first getting permission, but I wasn't going to do that this time. I started the car up, backed it out of the lot, and headed for the Thompson farm. I had to find out if Guennie was all right.

When I hit the dirt road, I turned on the brights. The road was so narrow I was only able to go about twenty miles per hour. I followed it around and around in the darkness until I was able to make out the Thompson barn and farmhouse. I pulled off the road into a clearing and turned off the engine. I was about to turn off the headlights when I realized if I did, I wouldn't be able to see a thing. I left them on so I could see where I was going.

The mosquitoes were especially robust tonight. They swarmed around me as I ran across the road and up to the wire fence. I looked for the spot where I had entered before. It took me a minute, but I located it. I squeezed under and found myself in an empty barnyard. There were no animals out. They all must be in the barn. I picked up the pace and hightailed it about a hundred yards to the farmhouse.

There was light coming from a couple of the windows. I wasn't sure if I was doing the right thing, but I needed to find out if Guennie was home and if she was all right. I knew I risked physical harm if the Thompson boys returned while I was here, but I had to chance it. I climbed the stairs and knocked on the back door. I waited a minute and knocked again. *She's gotta be home. She just has to.*

Another minute passed, and then I saw a figure

coming toward me. It had to be Guennie. She pulled back the curtains on the door and looked out. When she saw who it was, the expression on her face didn't suggest she was happy to see me. She rolled her eyes and shook her head. Then she opened the door.

"You must be crazy coming out here," she said as she stuck her head out and looked around. "They're gonna be home anytime now, and you can't be here."

"I just wanted to find out if you were all right, that's all."

"I'm fine. So just go, will you please?"

When she took a second look out the door, I could just faintly make out something red on the side of her face. I didn't know what made me do it, but I reached out and moved back her hair for a better look. She pulled away.

But I had seen the result of her father's brutal nature. There was a welt on the side of her face just below her ear.

"Did he do that to you?" I asked.

She sighed. "What do you think? He has ways of making his point. Now would you please just go. I don't want to see you get hurt."

I suddenly had a brainstorm. I pointed to the clearing where the headlights were still glowing.

"I have a car here. Why don't you come with me and we can sit in the car and talk."

She folded her arms and glared. "I know what you have on your mind. But it ain't happening. Got it?"

"I don't know what you're talking about. I just want to talk. That's all. I thought it might be safer in the car. We can drive down the road a little ways and turn the lights off. Then no one'll see us."

"And how long before you'll have your hands all over me?"

"I swear to God I won't lay a hand on you. I'm not like that. I promise."

She put her hands on her hips. "I got a better idea. Why don't you leave now before something bad happens."

I knew she was right. I knew if her dad and brothers found me here—with her, they'd beat the crap out of me. But there was just something about her that gave me the courage not to think twice about my own personal safety.

"I'm not leaving until you come with me," I said. "And that's final."

"Okay," she said. "Suit yourself." She slammed the door and walked away.

Uh-oh, I wasn't counting on that. I thought my ultimatum would convince her to join me. Apparently not. But I wasn't about to give up. I started banging on the door and didn't quit until she came back.

"Oh, my God, you are such a pest," she said.

"Listen, Guennie, come with me for ten minutes, tops. I just want to talk."

She threw her head back and let out a long sigh. "Ten minutes and not a minute more."

"Okay, great."

She pulled the door closed behind her and followed me across the barnyard and up to the fence.

When I looked back I noticed a small shed between the house and the barn. I pointed to it.

"What's in there?" I said.

"Believe me, you don't want to go in there," she said. "It's hot and smelly."

167

"What is it?"

"It's an outhouse," she said. "It smells awful, and it's like a hundred degrees in there in the summer."

"You mean—that's how you…"

She smiled. "We used to. We got indoor plumbing about three years ago."

I decided not to belabor the point. I bent down and pulled up the bottom wire so she could sneak through. Then I slithered through myself. I motioned for her to follow me to the car. I ran around to the passenger side and opened the door for her. I hadn't had a lot of practice being a gentleman on a date, but I knew that was a good move. I ran around to the driver's side and hopped in.

"Pull up about five hundred yards," she said. "There's a little gravel road you can turn off onto."

"Sounds good."

I turned the ignition and the car made this awful sound. The engine was straining to turn over in the worst way. What was wrong? Why now? And then it hit me. The battery. When I left the headlights on, it had been draining the battery. I kept trying. Oh, please, start up. I couldn't get caught out here by the Thompsons or by my dad.

I glanced at Guennie. She had a disgusted look on her face. This was not the best way to impress a girl. I continued at it. A couple of times it acted like it wanted to turn over, but then it sputtered out.

"Doesn't look good," she said calmly.

"Don't worry, I'll get it." I pushed the gas pedal and held it to the floor. Then I turned the key and prayed.

And just like that it started up.

I exhaled. "Told ya." I put the car in drive and turned onto the dirt path. I followed it past a lot of nothing—trees, shrubs, farm fields, and so on.

"Up there on your right," she said. "You see that opening?"

I was looking exactly where she was pointing, but I didn't see a thing. "Um…not exactly."

"Slow down," she said. "It's coming up."

And then I saw it—a fork in the road.

"Turn right, and then pull over on the side."

I followed her instructions. I turned off the engine—and the lights, this time.

"Okay, ten minutes," she said. "Go."

And suddenly I was tongue-tied. It was as if I was back at an Anton J. Cermak College Prep sock hop. I didn't know where to start. I was hoping she might kick things off and then I could just jump in.

"Well, if you have nothing to say," she said, "let's just turn around and go back."

And then I just spit it out. "I…I've never met anyone like you," I said.

"I don't mean to be rude," she said, "but what's the sense of getting to know one another when you'll be heading home in a couple of days? If you lived here, then maybe we'd get together."

I couldn't believe she had just said that. It was so awesome to hear. She could actually get interested in me if I lived here.

It didn't necessarily help things, but it was great for my ego.

Okay, I needed a good comebacker.

"That's why I wanted to get to know you," I said, "since we have so little time." Okay, now that sounded really good to me. I was hoping she would feel the same way.

She tilted her head and smiled. With the moon as our only light source, I was able to make out her profile. She was so beautiful.

"You seem like a sweet guy, Paulie Passero. But don't waste your time on someone like me. I'm damaged goods. Save yourself for a nice girl back home in Chicago."

"I'm not interested in girls back home. I'm interested in you. And what do you mean you're *damaged goods?* You're perfect."

She leaned back, put her head on the top of the seat, and extended her legs. "You don't know anything about me. If you did, you'd run for the hills and never look back."

"There's nothing you could tell me that would make me think any less of you."

Then, out of nowhere, she started to cry. She covered her face with her hands. "Just take me home."

"You said ten minutes," I said. "We still have time."

She turned toward me and just stared at me for a moment. Then she leaned over and buried her head in my chest. She was still crying.

My heart was racing. I didn't want to screw this up. I felt the urge to put my arms around her—not to get fresh, just to comfort her. She continued to sob. I decided to go for it. I reached around her with both arms and held her—first loosely, then tighter. It felt so great to have her in my arms.

At that moment, I was on top of the world. I could do this. I could really do this.

She raised her head slightly and looked into my eyes. Then she moved forward and pressed her lips against mine. They were so soft and moist. I didn't want this moment to end. I wanted to stay here forever. She lifted her head, smiled, and nuzzled it back into my chest. I just held her for what seemed like an eternity. It was actually more like a couple of minutes. She was breathing heavily. I could feel something beating. I wasn't sure if it was her heart or mine.

She lifted her head and moved back across the seat. "That was nice," she said.

"So what's so awful about you that would scare me away?" I said.

She shook her head. "No, I don't want anyone to know. I'm too ashamed."

"Have you told your dad, at least?" I asked.

Her head snapped back. "Tell him? He's the problem."

I reached out and took her hand. "What is it? What's so awful?"

She dropped her head. "What would you say if I told you I wasn't a virgin?"

"I wouldn't care."

"And what would you say if I told you I lost my virginity when I was thirteen?"

"I still wouldn't care."

"What would you say if I told you I had an abortion?"

I looked directly at her.

"Twice," she said.

This was some heavy-duty stuff she was telling me. Apparently this girl had gotten around. I thought about what she had said for a moment.

And I soon realized I didn't care. I really didn't. All these awful things could have happened to her and I would still want to be with her.

"None of it would matter. None of it. But what does that have to do with your father? Did he punish you or something when he found out?"

She raised her head and looked right into my eyes. "Don't you know what I'm trying to tell you?"

I didn't know. So what if she was a little frisky as a teenager. She wasn't the first girl to have done it when she was thirteen. That wasn't so terrible. What *was* she trying to tell me anyway?

"I know you must think I'm kind of dense, but I'm just not sure what you're telling me. I'm sorry."

"These things happened in my house. In my own bed. By someone who is never supposed to touch a daughter like that."

And then it hit me. Like a ton of bricks. "Your father? Your father did those things to you?"

She sighed. "He did those things, and he's still doing them. Now I won't blame you if you run and never come back."

"I'm not running anywhere. Except maybe to the sheriff, that is. What your father's doing to you is against the law. It's incest. It's *rape*. He should go to jail, and for a long time." I pulled her closer to me. "Guennie, listen, we have to go to the sheriff. We have to tell him. They'll arrest your dad. Then he can't get at you anymore."

She smiled as if resigned to her fate. "It's his word against mine. Nothing will happen. Nothing will ever happen. He'll just deny it. And then things will get worse. No, we can't go to the sheriff."

"Well, maybe you can't, but I can."

She grabbed my shoulder. "Paulie, don't. Please don't. Nothing will come of it. And when he finds out I told someone, he'll make me pay for it." She pulled back her hair to expose the welt on her face. "And this'll be nothing compared to what he'll do to me."

"I can't just sit back and let this happen to you. Someone has to do something."

She sat back, placed her hands in her lap, and looked at the floor. "I said something to a teacher a couple of years ago. A social worker visited our place. My dad was the perfect gentleman. And there was no way I was going to say anything in front of him. I still have marks from the belt he used on me that time."

I couldn't believe what this girl had to endure. It just wasn't right. I knew the more I brought up going to the sheriff, the more she would try to talk me out of it. I decided to tell her what she wanted to hear—that I would do nothing—but that was the last thing I was going to do.

"You're absolutely sure you don't want me to tell someone?"

"I'm sure," she said. "It would only make things worse."

I sighed. "Okay, but I don't like it."

She leaned over and kissed me on the cheek. "We'd better go back now. They could be home soon."

I squeezed her hand, started up the car, and turned the lights on. I backed up a few feet, then put the car in drive and proceeded down the dirt road. I wasn't going more than fifteen miles an hour. We drove for a couple of minutes.

"Pull over up there," she said. She reached over

and opened the car door.

"I'll walk you in," I said.

"No, you'd better go. It's not safe." She slid back over, leaned in, and kissed me on the mouth. It was a little longer than last time. I didn't want it to end. She pulled away and smiled. "Say hello to all your friends in Chicago for me." She hopped out and closed the door.

I rolled down the window. "This isn't goodbye. I'm going to see you again."

She slid under the wire fence and jumped to her feet. "Goodbye, Paulie Passero. Have a nice life." And she was gone.

I sat there for a minute and then continued on. When I got to the end of the dirt road where the paved road began, I saw a pair of headlights bearing down on me. The vehicle had to be going fifty miles per hour. I soon realized it was not going to slow down or stop. I swerved at the last second to avoid a pileup. As the vehicle passed me, I could see it was the Thompsons' pickup truck. One of the older brothers was in the driver's seat. What a moron. Seeing this dysfunctional family in action confirmed for me I had to tell the sheriff about the abuse at Guennie's home.

I pulled the car back onto the road and drove up the hill to my grandparents' place. I parked the car in the lot next to the house and walked up the front porch steps. I tried the door. Locked. I stepped back and looked around. There were no lights on in any room. I ran to the back door and tried it. Locked. Oh, great, now what? I jogged to the front door of the bar. Again locked. This was messing things up big time. My plan was to sneak upstairs, place the keys on top of the dresser in my dad's room, and then leave and head over to Uncle Buddy's. I couldn't just drive to Uncle Buddy's and come back in the morning. Then my dad would know I took the car—without permission. I didn't know what to do.

And then it hit me. Of course. I bent down, lifted the welcome mat, and pulled out a key. Yes! I unlocked the door, raced through the bar, tiptoed upstairs, and snuck into my dad's room. He appeared to be asleep. I ever so gently deposited the car keys on the dresser, and headed for the door. This was going to work out perfectly. I was about to step into the hallway when the lamp next to my dad's bed suddenly went on.

"Don't move a muscle, young man."

Chapter 16

Oh, no! I froze, then slowly turned to face my executioner. I looked at my dad's face. I wanted to see his expression. I could tell he was pissed.

"Do you mind telling me just what the hell is going on?"

"Um...I needed to borrow the car for a few minutes. And I didn't want to bother you, so I just took it."

"You didn't want to bother me? What kind of crap is that? Paulie, you had no business leaving this place without letting me or your uncle know."

"But I did tell him. I told Uncle Buddy where I was going."

He stood up and folded his arms. He was only wearing boxer shorts.

"Yes, your uncle tried to tell me some cock 'n' bull story about you going back to his place. I almost bought it until I noticed the car was gone. Do you want to tell me where you were?"

At that moment, I was puzzled. Should I attempt to BS him with some lame effort? Or should I tell him the truth? I opted for the former.

"I was bored and decided to go for a drive."

"At night, and in an area you know nothing about. Do you really expect me to believe that? I want the truth. Now."

I sighed. "Dad, it's a long story."

He sat back down on the bed. "Give me the *Reader's Digest* version."

I stared at my shoes. "I met this girl. She's the daughter of Mr. Thompson, the farmer down the dirt road. The same one who busted up the bar."

"Very nice," he said sarcastically. "Now you're cavorting with the enemy."

"It has nothing to do with that. As a matter of fact, he doesn't like me very much."

My dad shook his head. "So why in God's name are you hanging around with his daughter?"

"She's nothing like him. She's trying to get away from him." And then I decided to share all the dirt with my dad. "And we have to help her get away from him."

"What are you talking about?"

I wasn't exactly sure how to phrase it. "She told me he...he...is abusing her."

"What are you trying to say?"

I swallowed hard and let it fly. "Dad, he's having sex with his own daughter. It's *incest*. It's *rape*. We have to tell someone. We need to go to the sheriff's office and report him."

"And so why is this *our* problem? Why doesn't she go to the sheriff herself?"

"Because she's afraid to. She's afraid her dad'll beat her if she does. He's done it before."

My dad locked his jaw. "Paulie, I don't think this is any of our business. You seem to forget why we came here. You were supposed to say goodbye to your grandmother, not hang around with some floozie."

I lost it. "She's not some floozie! Don't say that!"

He moved in my direction. "Don't you ever raise

your voice to me again. Do you understand?"

I didn't say a word. He just didn't get it. He just didn't understand.

"Let me tell you something, young man. You are not to see this girl again. You're not to go to the sheriff's office and report anything. And you're not to leave this house. Do you understand?"

There was something I had to do, and he wasn't about to stop me. "Dad, I can't leave here knowing this girl is in trouble. I'm sorry, but I have to help her."

"Maybe you didn't hear me—"

I turned and walked out of the bedroom. I walked into the hallway and down the stairs. I could hear my dad yelling from the second-floor landing.

"Paulie! Paulie! You get back here right now!"

I ran into the kitchen, through a small supply room, and into the bar. I managed to bump into a stool and bang my knee. Oh, that smarted. Then I walked out the front door of the bar, bent down and retrieved the key from under the mat, and locked the door. I paused for a moment and looked out into the dark night sky. Now what should I do? I had left the car keys on the dresser in my dad's room, so I couldn't sleep in the Chevy. My only other option was Uncle Buddy. I would have to walk to his mobile home in the dark and hope he was there. Since the skies were overcast, there was little to no moonlight. This wouldn't be easy, but what choice did I have?

I moved over to the side of the road and started up the hill. I tried to remember the route Uncle Buddy had taken when he drove me to his place the other day. I broke into a jog and continued forward. As long as I could feel the stones under my feet, I knew I was on the shoulder of the road. I tried not to panic. My problems were tiny compared to Guennie's. My plan was to make it to Uncle Buddy's, and then first thing in the morning, I'd go to the sheriff's office and tell him about the abuse at the Thompson farm. My hopes were he would arrest her dad and put him in jail for a long time.

I pushed forward in the dark the best I could. When I reached Maple Lane, I was fairly certain I needed to turn right. I did so and followed it down the hill to the main road. A few minutes later, I came upon a bridge I remembered seeing before. I now had a pretty good idea where I was. I crossed the bridge and soon found myself in downtown Leroy. The streetlights on either side of Main Street would make the remainder of the trip a whole lot easier to navigate. I was only a couple blocks from Uncle Buddy's mobile home when I had a thought. I wondered if the sheriff's office was open right now. It just might be. Since crimes can happen at any time of the day or night, there was a pretty good chance someone would be there. I ran the three blocks to the office but found it empty and dark inside. I would have to wait until morning.

I continued my trek to Uncle Buddy's. I hoped he would be awake and wouldn't be upset with me for having put him on the spot earlier in the evening. I knocked on the front door and waited. I knocked again a minute later. Nothing. Then I decided to try the door. Maybe he had left it unlocked for me. I turned the knob, and to my delight, it opened.

The front room and the kitchen were dark. I turned on a lamp on one of the end tables. I needed to talk to Uncle Buddy about Guennie. I hoped he would support my decision to go to the sheriff's office.

Uncle Buddy's bedroom door was closed. I put my ear to the door and could swear I heard voices. I knocked lightly. No answer. I knocked again. Still nothing. So I decided to open it. When I did, I could hear what sounded like groans and someone breathing heavily. I flipped on the light.

What I saw I will never forget. Uncle Buddy was in his bed. He was naked. And his roommate, Jonathan, was naked and in the same bed. They were embracing. Oh, my God. Oh, my God. Uncle Buddy was a queer. He was a homosexual. It couldn't be. It just couldn't. I turned the light off and ran out.

"Paulie," he yelled.

I made it to the front door before he came out of his room. He was wearing a pair of jeans and no shirt. I began banging my head against the door. Why was this happening? Why? Why? Why? Everything was so messed up. I felt his hand on my shoulder. I pulled away.

"Paulie, we need to talk," he said.

"I have nothing to say to you," I replied. I didn't want to hear anything from him. Now I finally knew why my dad seemed disgusted whenever Uncle Buddy's name came up. And why the Thompsons referred to him as Tinkerbell. They knew his little secret. They knew he was living a double life. Why couldn't he be honest enough to tell me? This changed everything between us. I couldn't stay here knowing what I had seen. This was bad. Very bad.

"Please sit down," he said.

"No!"

"Let me explain."

"I don't want to hear anything from you."

"You're not being fair, Paulie."

I spun around. "Why couldn't you tell me? Why did I have to find out like this?"

He motioned for me to sit down on the couch. "You're right. I should have said something."

I reluctantly sat down.

"I have to be very careful who I tell. If the school board were to find out, I'd be out of a job. It's a secret I'm forced to keep. I would have told you eventually." He sat down in a chair across from me. "I need you to promise me you won't tell anyone about this. You owe me that. I've stuck my neck out for you more than once these last few days."

He was right. If it weren't for him, I wouldn't have been able to see Guennie. I did owe him something.

"I won't say anything."

"Do you promise?"

"Yes, I promise," I said without making eye contact.

He moved over to the couch and sat down next to me. "I thought we had a special bond—you and me. Nothing's changed, really. I'm still the same person."

I looked at him and shook my head. "Nothing's changed?"

"Paulie, I am who I am. This is how God made me. I didn't ask to have these feelings. They've been part of me my entire life. But very few people understand. That's why I keep it hidden."

"My entire life, I've been taught there's something wrong with being a..." I couldn't even say it.

"I'm a homosexual. Say it."

I stared at the floor. "Uncle Buddy, I really liked you. You were the only one I could trust. You seemed to understand me better than anyone else. You didn't criticize me for being a below-average student. You inspired me. I could never have read an entire book in a single day before I met you." I looked directly at him. "I don't want that to change."

"Neither do I. And it doesn't have to."

"But people say what you're doing is wrong," I said. "Who am I supposed to believe?"

"Believe *me*. I would never steer you wrong. If you hadn't seen what you did just now in the bedroom, would you think any less of me?"

"No."

"That's the only difference between you and me. Can you try to understand that?"

"I'll try."

"And that's all I can ask." He leaned over and put his arm around me.

I didn't know why, but right at that moment, I started to cry. What was wrong with me? This had never happened to me before.

"It's all right, Paulie."

"So many crazy things are happening to me right now. I don't think I can handle them."

He lifted my chin with his hand. "You can handle them. You're strong. You may not know it, but you are."

We talked for the next hour. He told me how difficult it was for him growing up. The teasing. The taunting. The more he explained his lifestyle to me, the more it made sense.

I started to question everything I had heard about people like him. If that was how you were made, if that was how you came out of the womb, then how could it be wrong? I didn't think I would ever get that image of him and Jonathan out of my head, but I had to try. That was part of his private life and it was none of my business.

We did eventually get around to the topic of Guennie and her dad. Uncle Buddy was very supportive. He agreed I should go to the sheriff's office in the morning and tell him what I knew.

I spent the rest of the night on Uncle Buddy's couch. I felt better about things. I tried to concentrate on Guennie and her situation. I rehearsed what I would tell the sheriff. I imagined him racing out to the farm, throwing handcuffs on Mr. Thompson, and hauling him off to jail. That would be so great. I could see Guennie hugging me and thanking me for putting an end to her nightmare.

Tomorrow would be a better day for all of us.

I just knew it.

Chapter 17

The next morning I awoke early. I wasn't sure what time the sheriff's office opened. I got up, toasted a bagel, poured myself a glass of milk, and sat alone at the kitchen table. I stared at the clock. It read 7:30. I went over the story I planned to tell the sheriff a dozen times. What if I couldn't convince him to investigate the matter? Then what? I didn't want to think about it. I wouldn't cross that bridge until it became necessary. I thought about Guennie. I thought about her kisses. I wanted to be with her so badly. I was pretty sure I was in love with her. If this wasn't love, then I didn't know what it was.

At 7:50 I cleaned up after myself and headed out. I walked the half mile or so into town. When I reached the sheriff's office, I looked through the window. I was glad to see him sitting at his desk. I walked in and introduced myself. I spotted his name on his desk.

"Sheriff Middleton, my name is Paulie Passero. My grandfather owns—"

"I know who you are, son," he said. "What can I do for you?"

I saw a chair opposite his desk. "Is it all right if I sit down?"

He waved me over. "So what brings you in here today?"

I had my story all memorized. I decided to let it fly.

"Sheriff, I'd like to report a crime—an ongoing crime that's been happening over and over again. I'm sure you're familiar—"

"Whoa, whoa, whoa," the sheriff said. "Slow down. What type of crime are we talking about? And who's the perpetrator?"

"I'm not exactly sure how to describe it. What do you call it when a father has sex with his sixteen-year-old daughter?"

He sat up in his chair and seemed more interested. "That would be incest. And statutory rape. So who's been doing this?"

"Mr. Thompson, the man with the farm down the dirt road over there." I pointed in the direction of the Happy Time Lounge.

"Travis Thompson? The one with the three boys who I warned you about the other day?"

"One and the same."

He stroked his forehead. "Are we talking about Guennie?"

I nodded.

"And how do you know this?"

"She told me," I said.

"She actually told you her father was having relations with her?" the sheriff said.

"Yes."

The sheriff got up from his desk and began pacing. "Paulie, these are some very serious allegations you're making."

"I understand that, but we have to do something. We have to get Guennie out of there before he abuses her any more."

"Why are you reporting this?" he said. "Why

hasn't Guennie come down here and told me these things?"

I stood up. "Because she's afraid to. If her father knew she'd told you, he'd beat her. He already has. She has the marks on her body to prove it."

The sheriff seemed to think to himself for a moment. Then he walked over to his desk and picked up the phone.

"Alice, if anybody wants me, I'll be over at the Travis Thompson farm." He hung up the phone. "I don't like accusing people of things they didn't do." He looked right at me. "You'd better be right, son."

"It's true," I said. "I guarantee it."

"Come on," he said.

I followed him outside. He pointed to the squad car. "Get in."

"I'm going with you?"

"What? You don't want to?"

"No, I do. I do." I opened the passenger door and climbed in. There was a radio on the dash and a microphone on the seat. There were sure a lot more bells and whistles in this car than we had in the Bel Air. There was a see-through metal barrier that separated the front seat from the back. That had to be so the criminals couldn't get at the sheriff. I imagined Thompson sitting back there.

The sheriff started up the car, made a U-turn, and hit the gas.

I held on to the door handle and we raced over the bridge, up Maple, and down Irving Road. We slowed down somewhat when we hit the dirt road. A couple of minutes later, we arrived at the Thompson farm. The sheriff pulled up to a gate with a padlock on it. One of

Guennie's brothers was in the barnyard. He stopped what he was doing and put his hands on his hips. The sheriff exited the vehicle and motioned for the boy to unlock the gate. The boy made a face and slowly walked into the farmhouse. A minute or so later, he came back out with a key in his hand and said something to the sheriff. I rolled down the window to hear what they were saying.

"None of your business," the sheriff said. "I need to talk to your father."

"He's busy now. He can't talk."

"He'll see me. Now unlock this gate. Now."

The boy reluctantly opened the padlock.

The sheriff looked in my direction. "Stay in the car." He glared at the Thompson boy and then glanced back at me. "And lock the doors."

I rolled up the window and reached around and pushed down the locks on all four doors. I watched as the sheriff followed the boy across the barnyard and into the house. He looked familiar. I was pretty sure his name was Johnny. I tried to imagine what was happening in there. I tried to picture the expression on Thompson's face when the sheriff accused him of abusing his daughter. In a way, I wished I could have been in there to witness it. And in a way I was glad I was in here. I thought about Guennie. If she was around and heard the charges, she would know they came from me. I wasn't sure how she would react. Would she be really upset? I prayed she wouldn't. I knew I had done the right thing. I only hoped everything worked out okay.

A few seconds later, I saw the brother I had seen earlier. He was now walking toward the police car. The other two brothers were close behind. They came out through the gate and walked right toward me. I double-checked to make sure all the doors were locked. The boys came up to the car, bent down and looked in.

"Come out of there, you faggot," one of them said.

My heart began to race. *Please hurry, Sheriff.* I didn't know what these jerks might do. And I didn't want to find out. The same boy started banging on the passenger side window.

"I said come out of there—now."

I looked down. I didn't want to make eye contact.

A second brother crawled on top of the hood and began pounding on the windshield with his fists. He spit on the glass and smeared it around with his hand.

"That's for you," he yelled.

The third brother hopped up on the trunk and began jumping on it. The entire vehicle began bouncing up and down. These guys were nuts.

I closed my eyes and kept my head down like I was staring at the floor. The assailants continued their assault for the next several minutes. I never once gave them the satisfaction of looking at them. I just wanted to survive this barrage. I wanted so badly to raise my head, smile, and give them the finger. I knew it would make them even crazier. But I didn't know what they'd do, so I decided to lay low, taking a peek once in a while to see what they were going to do next.

"If you don't come out, then we're coming in," the one on the hood said. "Go get the crowbar in the barn," he told the youngest brother.

Crowbar? Oh no. They were going to break the windows and drag me out. *Sheriff! Please hurry!*

The younger one returned moments later carrying a

long metal rod. "Couldn't find the crowbar, but I got this."

"That'll do the trick," the other one said. He grabbed the rod from his brother, held it like a baseball bat, and was just about to make contact with the windshield when a voice froze him in his tracks. It got my attention as well.

"Get the hell off that car right now," the sheriff ordered. He was holding his baton at arm's length.

"We wasn't doin' anything, Sheriff," the oldest boy said. "We was just trying to get to know your friend a little better. That's all."

"Move away from the vehicle—now!"

The middle brother held his hands up. "Okay, okay, you don't have to yell." The three backed away from the car and headed toward the gate.

The sheriff walked briskly in the direction of the car. He fumbled momentarily for his keys and unlocked the driver's side door. He never took his eyes off the brothers. He hopped in, pulled the door closed, and locked it. He started the engine, backed up, and headed down the road. He never once spoke. When we came to the end of the dirt road where the pavement began, he slowed down, climbed the hill, and stopped directly in front of my grandparents' house. He pointed to the door.

"Out," he said.

I was confused. I didn't know what was happening. I opened the door and stopped.

"Sheriff, what happened back there?"

He sighed. "Nothing happened back there. Now would you please exit the vehicle."

"I don't get it. What did Thompson say when you

accused him of abusing Guennie?"

The sheriff cocked his head. "He said he didn't do it."

"Well, what else did you expect him to say? Of course, he would say that. Did you ask Guennie?"

"Yes."

"And what did she say?"

He turned his body toward me. "She said nothing happened."

"What?"

"She said her father never touched her."

I shook my head. "She's lying. She's afraid of what he'll do to her if she admits to it."

"Or…she was telling me the truth. I should never have let you talk me into this."

"We have to go back there right now," I said.

"What? Are you crazy? Just get out."

"He's beating her as we speak, and you're not going to do anything about it?"

"We don't know that."

I pounded on the dashboard. "*I* know that." I pulled the door closed. "Are you really going to take the chance nothing's happening right now? What kind of a sheriff are you anyway? One who lets people beat the crap out of their own kids while you look the other way?"

He let out a long sigh.

"Sheriff, please. We have to hurry. Guennie's in trouble."

He threw his head back, groaned, and put the car in reverse. "I don't know why the hell I'm listening to you. I must be crazy."

He moved the lever on the column and roared

down the road. We kicked up dust when we hit the dirt. I held on for dear life as we zigged and zagged all the way back to the Thompson farm. We skidded to a stop at the front gate. It was still unlocked. The sheriff threw open his door.

"This time you're coming with me so you can see for yourself."

I opened the door slowly. I wasn't sure about this. I wondered what Guennie's brothers would do to me. I needed to stick close to the sheriff as best I could. I followed him through the gate, across the barnyard, and up the stairs to the farmhouse.

The sheriff rapped on the front door. The oldest brother opened it. When he saw me, he smiled, and motioned for the other brothers to join him.

"Well, what do we have here?" he said.

"I need to speak to your father," the sheriff said.

The boy looked at me, winked, and disappeared momentarily. I knew he was trying to intimidate me. And it was working. When he returned, his father was with him.

"What is it this time, Fred?" Mr. Thompson said disgustedly.

"I have one more question for your daughter," the sheriff said. "Can you get her for me?"

"I'm...I'm...I'm afraid she's not here," Thompson said.

"She was here five minutes ago," the sheriff said.

Mr. Thompson rubbed his unshaven face. "She's...at a friend's house."

"What's her friend's name and where does she live?" the sheriff said.

Thompson shook his head. "I'm afraid I don't

know that. Hard to keep track of who her friends are these days. Sorry, you'll have to come back later." He started to close the door.

The sheriff stuck his foot between the door and the jamb. "Travis, I want to see her right now."

"I told you she's not here."

"Then you won't mind if I come in and take a look for myself?" the sheriff said.

Thompson filled the doorway blocking our entrance. "I do mind."

"What have you done to her?" I said. I couldn't help myself. I just spit it out.

"Get the hell off my property, both of you. Fred, you're not getting in here without a search warrant." Thompson smiled. "Yeah, I know my rights."

The sheriff sighed. "Okay, then, I'll be back. And you'd better produce her."

"Go away." Thompson slammed the door shut.

"Now what?" I said.

The sheriff motioned for me to follow him. We hustled back to the car and jumped in. The sheriff spun the vehicle around and we tore out of there. I looked back through the rear windshield and all I could see was a cloud of dust. Pretty soon we hit the paved road and he accelerated.

"Where are we headed?" I asked.

"County seat," the sheriff said. "That's where the judge is. And that's where we'll get our search warrant."

"So you believe me now?"

"It appears he's done something to that girl. I just hope we're not too late."

Chapter 18

It took us the better part of a half hour to drive to Blain City, the Van Dyke County seat. I waited outside in the car while Sheriff Middleton was in the courthouse trying to convince a judge to sign a warrant to search the Thompson property. People walking by the squad car gave me funny looks. I suppose they thought I was a criminal. I mean—who else besides a police officer sits in one of these cars? I just smiled and nodded to anyone who stared at me. I wanted them to know I was at least a cordial prisoner. Most folks looked away and shook their heads.

A few minutes later, the sheriff came running down the courthouse steps with something in his hand. He jumped in the car, put it in gear, and we were off.

"You got it?" I asked.

He nodded.

"Sheriff, does that piece of paper give us the right to search the entire property, not just the house?"

"You been watching too many cop shows," he said.

"Well, I was just thinking about the barn. They might hide her in there."

He picked up the warrant off the seat and waved it. "We can look everywhere on that property, although if Thompson's smart, he'll have moved her somewhere else. I only hope we're not wasting our time."

I was thinking the same thing. Who in his right

mind would leave his victim in plain sight? There must be some hiding places on that farm, I thought, and we'd have to find them. I was hoping, praying, Guennie was all right. The fact her father had refused to let us see her indicated he had put some new marks on her. Every time I thought about him raising his hand to her it made me crazy. I wanted to kill him for what he had done. But seeing him in jail would have to do.

We moved through the back roads of Van Dyke County at breakneck speeds. It was nice to know the sheriff finally believed me. Why else would he have taken the time to get the search warrant? I only hoped we could find her.

And then I got to thinking about other things. I wondered how angry my dad was with me. I had defied him and walked out. It wouldn't be pretty when we met up again. But I couldn't concentrate on that right now. There were other more pressing issues on my mind. As important as saving Guennie was, I thought again of that scene in Uncle Buddy's bedroom, the one with him and Jonathan in bed. I shook my head. I wanted to remove that image from my mind, but nothing I did seemed to work.

I tried to convince myself there was nothing unnatural about two men making love, but everything I'd heard and read up until that point had told me differently. I wanted to understand how homosexuals thought and acted and why they did what they did. But it was all so foreign to me that it was hard to comprehend. I would just have to believe in Uncle Buddy.

No man had ever been that gentle and understanding with me. No man had ever cared as much about my education before. No man had encouraged me the way he did. No man had ever drawn out from me my deepest and darkest feelings about girls. Uncle Buddy was a special man. Sure, he was different in some ways. But most of those ways were of a private nature. They didn't concern anyone else. He had allowed me into his world—a world he had kept secret from everyone. I needed to keep that secret for as long as Uncle Buddy wanted me to. There was no way I would breach his confidence.

Before I realized it, we were on the outskirts of Leroy. We'd be at the Thompson farm in minutes. I wondered if the sheriff would want me to accompany him again once we got there. Even if it meant getting a little roughed up, I wanted to be there when we found Guennie. I wanted her to know she was safe and that no one would ever hurt her again.

We flew by the Happy Time Lounge and were on the dirt road in record time. We arrived at the Thompson farm moments later. This time the gate was locked, and there was no one around to unlock it for us. The sheriff laid on the horn for several seconds hoping to draw someone out of the house. It didn't work. Then he activated the siren. It sounded for a good minute before he turned it off.

The sheriff sighed.

"What are we gonna do?" I said. "Who knows what he's doing to her right now?"

The sheriff thought to himself for a moment. Then he looked over his shoulder, put the car in reverse, and backed up a few yards.

"Hold onto your seat, Paulie. We're goin' in."

Sheriff Middleton gripped the steering wheel and

proceeded to floor the squad car. We were headed right for the gate at top speed. I grabbed the door handle and closed my eyes. A second later, I heard a loud crash and felt myself being thrown backward against the seat. Wood, metal, and glass pelted the windshield. We had successfully broken through the padlocked gate. The sheriff stopped the car and reached into the back seat. He handed me a flashlight.

"Here, we might need this," he said.

We both hopped out of the car.

I watched the sheriff as he surveyed the area. You could tell he wanted to be prepared for anything—even an ambush. We walked across the barnyard and up the front steps. The sheriff rapped on the door—first gently, then forcibly.

"You're not welcome here," a voice called out. It was Thompson.

"I've got the search warrant, Travis. Open the door." But no one appeared. "Don't make me break this door down," the sheriff said. Again there were no sounds from within. "This is your last warning."

The sheriff waited a few seconds and then he handed me the search warrant. He stepped back and put his shoulder into the door. It budged a little, and I could hear wood cracking from the frame. He did it again. And then a third time. With that final blow, the door flew open and crashed against a counter in the kitchen. "Don't make this more difficult than it has to be."

And then a figure appeared in the doorway that led into the rest of the house. It was Thompson. He was pointing his finger at the outside door.

"The county's gonna pay for that, Fred."

"Where is she?" the sheriff asked.

"I told you before she's not here. There's no sense in looking."

As we stood there waiting to search the home, I couldn't help but look around. The room was filthy. There was garbage on the counters and the floor. Paint was peeling from the ceiling and the walls. Dirty pots and pans and dishes filled the sink. There was what looked like a dead chicken on the table. And the stench was nauseating.

I followed the sheriff as he pushed his way past Thompson and entered each room. Every one was dirtier than the last. The bedroom where I assumed the boys slept was indescribable. There were bare mattresses on the floor. Springs and stuffing shot out from each one. I wanted to hold my nose so badly, but I didn't want it to seem obvious. I tried breathing through my mouth as best I could. We looked in each closet, in the pantry, under beds, and behind each piece of furniture. Guennie was nowhere in sight. At one point I spotted an opening that seemed to lead to an attic. The sheriff pushed a dresser under the opening and climbed on top of it.

"Paulie, hand me the flashlight."

I'd almost forgotten I was carrying it. I tossed it up to him. Seconds later he disappeared into the attic.

And suddenly all three brothers were standing in the doorway.

"Now look what we have here," the oldest one said. "And he's all alone with nobody to protect him."

"I'm not lookin' for any trouble, guys," I said.

Thompson pushed his way into the room. "Any trouble? You're making a whole lot of it, boy. I wish you would just go back where you came from."

I knew any answer would provoke him further. I just stood there and prayed the sheriff would quickly reappear.

"You want us to teach him a lesson, Pa?" another brother said.

"I'd like nothing better," Thompson said.

Right at that moment, I was more scared than I could ever remember. It was four against one. I didn't stand a chance. The only time I could ever remember fighting anyone was when I was in fourth grade. There was a kid named Marty Landecky who lived across the alley from us. Marty was a mouthy kid who was always getting into trouble. I couldn't remember why we were friends. And one summer afternoon we found ourselves pitted against one another in a wrestling match in our back yard. It started out relatively friendly, but when one of my elbows whacked Marty across the mouth, it became an all-out brawl with punching and kicking, and both of us ended up with blood dripping from our faces. It was the last time Marty and I played together. And it was the last time I could remember raising my hand against another person.

I don't recall who hit me first, but the Thompson boys were on me in a flash. Initially I tried just holding them off, but when someone's fist landed on my right ear, something snapped in me. Call it self-preservation or just wanting badly to retaliate, but I started swinging. Most of my punches landed somewhere on the body parts of my enemies. Since they were all over me, that wasn't a difficult task. At one point I was on the floor, on my back, and someone was sitting on me. I knew I was in trouble unless I was able to spin around and face the floor. I knew it would be better to be taking punches to the back of my head than to my face. But before I was able to make that move, the sheriff jumped down from the attic onto the dresser and then onto the floor. He began pulling each brother off me, not before each of them took one final shot. Likewise, I twisted around and began flailing my arms with the hope of making contact. I did, and then I heard a groan from one of the brothers.

"Get out of this room right now," the sheriff shouted, "before I arrest each one of you."

"Your boy started it," Thompson said. "We was just defending ourselves."

"Yeah, I'll bet," the sheriff said.

Blood was dripping from the nose of the shortest brother. He wiped off some of it and looked at his hand.

"You're gonna pay for this, kid," he said.

Did I do that, I wondered? I thought about it for a moment. *Hell, yes. I bloodied a guy's nose. Well, that'll show 'em.*

The Thompson clan backed out of the room, and the sheriff helped me to my feet.

"I'm sorry about that, Paulie. I shouldn't have left you alone. Are you all right?"

My body ached all over. I couldn't straighten up. I felt like I needed to vomit right there.

"I'm okay, I think."

"C'mon, let's go check the barn," he said.

I felt my back crack as I righted myself. I wasn't going to give Guennie's brothers the satisfaction of seeing me in pain. I would act as if none of their blows had made a difference. I smiled confidently as we walked out of the bedroom, through the kitchen, and out the door.

"Come back for more," one of them yelled out. The others started laughing.

I could taste blood in my mouth, but it seemed as if all my teeth were still in place. I wiped my nose with my hand and saw it was bleeding too. As we passed the boys, I realized that for the first time I wasn't afraid, for some reason. Maybe it was because I had taken their best shot, and I had survived. Don't get me wrong. I wasn't in any hurry to repeat that incident, but I knew if it did occur again, I would enter it with more confidence.

I followed the sheriff down the porch stairs, across the grass and dirt, and into the barn. We began checking each stall for Guennie. Some of the occupants, namely a horse, two dairy cows, and a goat, were less than cooperative and voiced their disapproval as we invaded their space. When a search of the ground floor produced no signs of life, I volunteered to climb the makeshift ladder and inspect the loft. This time I remembered the broken rung as I made my way to the second level. I immediately looked behind the bales of hay Guennie and I had hidden behind earlier in the week. No one there. Then I walked from one side of the loft to the other. Again, no luck. When I climbed down, I shook my head at the sheriff.

"Unfortunately, that's what I was expecting," he said.

We stepped out into the barnyard and stood there surveying the area for a few moments. We were looking at deserted open fields, some for grazing, some for crops.

"All we can do is stop at some of the other farms in the area and ask them to keep their eyes open for the girl," the sheriff said. "I'm not sure what else we can do at this point."

I hated giving up. Did Thompson have her so well hidden I would never see her again? The thought made me ill. I just couldn't leave Leroy without seeing her one more time. If we never found her, and since it was doubtful I'd be back here in the near future, I would always wonder what happened and if she was all right.

"Let's go," the sheriff said.

I reluctantly trudged back toward the car with the feeling I had somehow failed Guennie. Who else would be her advocate out here? And then suddenly I thought of something.

"The outhouse!" I yelled.

"What?"

I pointed. "See, over there behind the barn. The outhouse. Maybe she's in there."

"It's so hot in those old sheds, it's doubtful anyone could survive if left there for a few hours."

"That's why we have to check it," I said.

The sheriff shook his head. "All right, whatever."

I ran over to the outhouse and found a padlock on the front door. "It's locked."

Just then Thompson appeared on the porch. "Get away from there," he said. "There's nothing in there."

"I need the key for this, Travis," the sheriff said.

"Ain't got it. Lost it years ago."

Guennie's brothers now appeared on the porch.

"What's he doin' over there?" the youngest one asked his father.

"Snoopin' around where he don't belong," Thompson said.

The sheriff reached into his pocket and dug out the

keys to the squad car. He handed them to me.

"There's a bolt cutter in the trunk," he whispered. "Go get it."

I ran past the house and the barn before reaching the car. I opened the trunk, looked around, and spotted the bolt cutter. It was heavy, with red handles and gray cutting blades. I grabbed it and closed the trunk. As I was about to make my way back to the outhouse, I noticed the Thompson boys were blocking my path.

"Let him through," the sheriff yelled.

The boys ignored the warning. I knew every moment that passed spelled trouble for Guennie if she was in that hot shed. Without hesitating, I plowed through the boys. As they attempted to land punches, I began swinging the bolt cutter. I spun around like a top, keeping them at bay as I made my way across the barnyard and up to the outhouse. I handed the tool to the sheriff as the boys backed off. One of them ran back onto the porch, said something to his father, and then went inside the house.

The sheriff meanwhile positioned the bolt cutter around the shackle and squeezed. The padlock snapped in two and fell to the ground. He immediately turned on his flashlight, opened the door, and entered the outhouse. The door slammed shut behind him. I reached over and re-opened the door just as the sheriff emerged with Guennie in his arms. I couldn't believe it. We had found her.

"We gotta get her to a hospital," he said.

I could see her right eye was swollen shut and her bottom lip was puffy, courtesy of her old man. Finally, that bastard would get what was coming to him. I picked up the bolt cutter and hustled to the car just ahead of the sheriff.

"Leave that girl be," Thompson yelled out. "You can't take her."

The sheriff said nothing. I opened the back door and helped him slide her onto the seat.

"Can I ride with her?" I asked.

Sheriff Middleton nodded.

I got into the back seat and lifted her head. I placed it in my lap. Her skin was burning up. She was groggy and breathing heavily. When she opened her eyes and saw me, she covered up her face with her hands.

"Don't look. Don't look at me. I'm so ugly."

I held her tightly. "You're so beautiful," I said.

Before the sheriff was able to get back into the driver's seat, Thompson made one last effort to keep us from removing his daughter from the farm. He was still standing on the porch, but now he was holding a rifle.

"I'll drop you where you stand, Fred," he said. "Leave the girl and go."

"Don't do something stupid, Travis," the sheriff said. "Just put the gun down and go inside."

When the sheriff opened the door, a shot rang out and the Mars light on top of the squad car shattered. The sheriff shielded himself from the flying glass and jumped into the car. He reached into his pocket for the keys and stopped.

"Paulie, the keys! I need the car keys!"

I had completely forgotten. I had used them to open the trunk and forgot to give them back.

A second gunshot pierced the front windshield of the car.

"He's a lunatic!" the sheriff said. He turned to us. "Get down!"

I dug into my pocket for the keys, reached over the seat, and handed them to the sheriff.

A third shot bounced off the hood. Still bent down, I heard the engine turn over and the car lunged in reverse.

Another shot rang out. This one traveled right through the back seat, shattering both windows. If I'd been sitting up, I'd have been a goner. The car then jerked forward, tires screeching, and I sensed we were safe.

Chapter 19

It took us about thirty minutes to get to Van Dyke Hospital in Blain City. When we arrived, two attendants came out to the car with a gurney. Guennie waved them off. She wanted to walk in by herself. I had my arm around her the entire time as we made our way to the emergency room.

The nurse who greeted us took Guennie into a partitioned area and asked me to sit in the waiting room. From my vantage point, I could see the sheriff on the phone for several minutes. Occasionally he would cover up the mouthpiece and speak to a doctor or nurse behind the glass. Then he returned to his call. His movements were animated. I could only guess he was calling in reinforcements to accompany him back to the farm to arrest Travis Thompson. With him in jail, Guennie would have nothing to fear.

While I sat there, I had a lot of time to think. I hoped my dad would understand why I had walked out on him. I couldn't just leave her there in that living hell. I would have to ask the sheriff to speak to him for me and explain the seriousness of the situation. Maybe then he would back off and give me a pass.

In the last couple of days, I hadn't really kept up on my grandmother's condition. I hoped when her time came she would die peacefully and painlessly. Once we made sure Guennie was in good hands, I would make it a point to visit Grandma for an official goodbye. It made me happy to think she had awoken that one time and spoken to me, even though no one else believed me.

"Excuse me," a nurse said. She had apparently been trying to get my attention.

"Yes."

"She'd like to see you," she said.

"Oh, okay."

I followed the nurse back into the emergency room area. When I found Guennie, she was sitting up on a bed. She wasn't nearly as red and flushed as she had been when the sheriff had carried her out of that shed. Her eye had been cleaned up and was now partially open. She was holding an ice pack on her lip. When she saw me, she started to cry. I put my arms around her.

"Nobody's going to hurt you anymore," I said.

"What do you suppose is going to happen to my father?"

"They're going to arrest him and put him in jail. He tried to kill us. Not to mention what he did to you."

She set the ice pack down on the bed. "Good. That's where he belongs."

The nurse was right outside the partitioned area, talking to the sheriff. I slid over and positioned myself close enough to hear their conversation.

"We did a pelvic exam on the girl," she said. "There was inflammation and vaginal tearing. Sheriff, she was definitely the victim of abuse. Do you know who did this to her?"

He nodded. "I do. And we're about to arrest him— for that and for a host of other offenses."

"Well, that's good to hear," the nurse said. "You

can talk to her now if you like."

"Thank you."

I hurried back over to Guennie before the sheriff entered. When he did, he set his hat down on the edge of the bed. He pulled up a chair and sat down next to her.

"Guennie, are you now prepared to tell me the truth?"

"Yes, I'm sorry I lied to you. I didn't know what he'd do to me if I told you about it."

"For the record, it was your father who abused you, correct?"

"Yes."

"Did any of your brothers do the same?"

"No, but I could tell it was just a matter of time before one of them did," she said. "Sheriff, if you arrest my dad, please don't send me back there with them."

"We won't do that to you, Guennie, but we have to find a place for you to live for a while. I'm working on that. I've made a few calls, and I'm waiting to hear back. For tonight, I'm going to bring you to my sister's home. She said it would be okay to bring you over. She has two daughters. I think one of them is your age. She might have even been in your class. Corinne Samuelson?"

"I know Corinne," she said. "She's a nice girl."

"I hope you'll be comfortable there until we can find you a permanent home."

"So I'll never have to go back to the farm?"

"I've been on the phone with the county's Department of Children and Family Services. We'll try to have you placed with a foster family until at least your eighteenth birthday. Does that sound okay?"

She teared up. "It sounds wonderful," she said. "Sheriff, do you think I'll be able to go back to school?"

"I don't see why not. If you want to, you should be able to."

She grinned. "Thank you."

The nurse stuck her head in. "Sheriff, there's a call for you."

"Excuse me," he said to Guennie as he walked into the hallway.

I turned to Guennie. "See, I told you everything was going to work out."

She was beaming. "I can't believe I'll be able to finish high school. And then maybe...college, even." She grabbed my shoulders. "Paulie, you have to go to college. Don't miss out on that opportunity."

"I'll think about it."

"Then make sure you do whatever you have to do to get in. I can tell you're a smart kid. You'll get into a college if you want to. But only if you want to."

The sheriff returned. His expression was grim. "Paulie, we need to go...right away. Guennie, my sister will be here in about a half hour to pick you up." He nodded at me. "Let's go."

I didn't know if this was goodbye for now or permanently. When would I see her again? This wasn't how I wanted things to end.

"Sheriff, could I have a minute?" I said.

"No, there's no time." And then he seemed to understand why this was so hard for me. "Paulie, you'll be able to see Guennie. My sister's house is about a half mile from my office. You can walk there. Now, c'mon."

I waved to her. She smiled and did the same. I couldn't wait to see her again. I ran out and caught up with the sheriff. He was already out the front door.

"What's so urgent, Sheriff?"

"Get in."

I hopped in the passenger seat and we were off.

"I just got a call from dispatch," he said. "There's a fire at your grandfather's tavern."

"A fire? Is everyone okay?"

"I don't have all the information, but it appears everyone got out safely."

"Even my grandmother? She's bedridden."

He sighed. "To be perfectly honest, I don't know about her. But if the firemen were told there was someone in one of the bedrooms, I'm sure they would have gotten her out."

I was having a hard time breathing. I was praying everyone was okay.

"Do you know how it started?" I asked.

"It appears someone threw a Molotov cocktail through the front window."

I couldn't believe it. "Who would do such—" And then it hit me. "I don't think it would take a genius to figure out who was behind this."

"Innocent until proven guilty," the sheriff said, "although I have the same suspicions."

This was turning out to be a pretty violent week. I only hoped everyone was okay. I couldn't bear to think anyone might have been injured. And then I thought about the fact it might have been my fault all of this took place. It was clear the Thompson boys were behind the fire.

And if I had never pursued Guennie, it's doubtful

any of this would have happened. I was feeling responsible. And guilty.

"Sheriff?"

"Yeah."

"I'm beginning to think all of the bad things that have happened are because of me."

"What are you talking about?"

I looked out the window for a moment. "If I hadn't tried to get to know Guennie, then her brothers would have no reason to set the fire."

"Son, don't think like that. You did a very brave thing. Without your help, that girl would have continued to suffer every day. You helped save her from a lifetime of misery."

It was comforting to hear those words, but they wouldn't make me feel any better until I knew if everyone got out.

The sheriff reached over and patted me on the shoulder. "You have nothing to feel guilty about."

We didn't talk for the next twenty or so minutes. When we were entering the outskirts of Leroy, I could see smoke rising from the direction of my grandparents' home. That wasn't a good feeling. My mouth was dry. I felt lightheaded. *Oh, God, please help everyone to be all right.* We raced down Irving Road and could see emergency vehicles up ahead. The sheriff slowed down and eventually stopped at a roadblock. The police had kept any cars from entering the area. The sheriff rolled his window down and a uniformed officer came over.

"What are the damages, Hugh?" the sheriff asked.

"We think we got everyone out. There's a woman who's suffering from smoke inhalation. She's getting oxygen now. I think she'll be okay."

"What about the structure?"

"The bar's a total loss. They're trying to save the house as we speak."

The officer pointed to the shattered windows and broken light on top of the car. "What happened here?"

"It's a long story," the sheriff said. "I'm going to need some assistance bringing in a suspect when things quiet down around here."

"Sure, just let me know."

The sheriff pointed to me. "This boy has family down there. Can you let us through?"

The officer nodded. He proceeded to move the wooden horses blocking the road and waved us through.

The squad car crept forward. The closer we got, the stronger the smell of smoke.

"That should make you feel a little better," the sheriff said.

I smiled. I wouldn't relax until everyone was accounted for. The woman the officer was describing had to be either Aunt Gloria or my grandmother. I was hoping it was Aunt Gloria—not because I wish any ill on her but because I thought she would be better able to handle the smoke.

As we inched forward, I could see the flames coming from the roof of the bar. Firefighters were pouring water on it from two different angles. I could see three fire trucks and a pair of ambulances. I looked around for my dad and the others. I didn't see them right away.

"Sheriff, can I get out?"

"All right, but stay back."

"Okay." I hopped out of the car and walked toward

the emergency vehicles. As I got closer, I could see Aunt Gloria sitting in the back of one of the ambulances. She was holding an oxygen mask over her nose and mouth. She appeared to be okay other than that. Then I spotted my grandmother in the back of the other ambulance. She still seemed to be unconscious. I continued searching for the others. I found my grandfather sitting in the back seat of a police car. I went over to see if he was all right. The back door was open.

"Gramps, are you okay?"

He smiled, pulled me closer, and hugged me. "Paulie, thank God you're okay. We weren't sure where you were. I was afraid you were inside somewhere." He squeezed me.

"Where's my dad and Uncle Buddy?"

He pointed to our car, still parked in the lot next door. They were both standing next to it. I ran over to them. Uncle Buddy spotted me first.

"Paulie," he said as he threw his arms around me. "Were you with the sheriff?"

"Yeah."

"What happened with Guennie?" he asked.

"We found her locked in an outhouse. She was pretty messed up. But we took her to the hospital, and it looks like she's going to be fine."

"And her dad? What happened to him?"

"He was shooting at us when we tried to take Guennie away. He's gonna be arrested soon."

"Oh, my God, you're kidding. Well, I'm glad you're all right."

The entire time I was talking to Uncle Buddy, my dad just stood there with his arms folded. I was watching him out of the corner of my eye. He was expressionless. I couldn't read him. I took a step in his direction.

"Dad, I'm sorry about walking out on you. But I had to. This girl was in real trouble, and we got her out of a bad situation."

"So it sounds like she's okay, and her dad's headed to jail?"

"It looks that way."

"Paulie, I understand now why you did what you did, but we'll need to have a serious conversation about it on the drive home."

The drive home? Oh, no. "We're leaving?"

"Your grandmother's organs have shut down. She has maybe hours left. Figure on leaving in the next two or three days. I'll get you back before school starts. Don't worry."

"I'm not worried about that."

My dad pointed to the ambulance holding my grandmother. "Maybe you should say your goodbyes."

I walked over to the ambulance with my dad following closely behind. There was a paramedic standing just outside.

"Can I go in there for a minute?"

He nodded and stepped away.

I crawled in on one side of the gurney holding my grandmother and knelt down next to her. Her hands were at her sides. I picked up one and held it. I wasn't exactly sure what I should be saying to a dying woman I had only met days before, but I needed to do this for my dad. I closed my eyes and said a prayer.

When I opened them, my dad was on the other side of the gurney. He was staring at her with a pained expression on his face. I felt bad for him.

Then I noticed something strange happening. My grandmother turned her head in my direction and opened her eyes just slightly. She squeezed my hand. My dad's eyes widened.

"Paulie, she said. "My only grandson." My dad was speechless.

She turned her head to him. She opened her hand for him to hold onto. He grabbed it.

"My Peter. My Peter. I told Papa you would come back. I told him." There were tears streaming down my dad's face.

"I'm here, Mama. I'm here."

She smiled. Seconds later I could feel her grip go limp. Her eyes closed. Her chest heaved momentarily, and then dropped. Her head fell to the side, and she appeared lifeless.

"We need some help in here," my dad yelled.

I slid out to make way for the paramedic. He jumped in and felt for the pulse in her wrist, and then her neck. He grabbed a stethoscope and listened to her heart, and then he turned to my dad and shook his head.

My dad leaned forward. His forehead was now resting on my grandmother's chest. He seemed to be maintaining his composure. He lifted his head and kissed her on the cheek. He looked back at me.

"She's gone, Paulie. She's gone."

I wasn't sure what to say. I just stood there.

"So she did speak to you earlier," he said. "I'm sorry for not believing you. I should have known better."

"It's okay, Dad."

He crawled out of the ambulance and motioned for

Uncle Buddy to come over. He whispered something into his ear. Uncle Buddy stepped into the back of the ambulance. My dad walked over to where Aunt Gloria was seated. She was still holding the oxygen mask. I couldn't hear what he said to her, but she dropped the mask and closed her eyes. My dad stepped back and looked over to where my grandfather was sitting in the police car.

"This is going to be the tough one," he said to me. "Your grandfather has taken a liking to you. Maybe you should be with him when I tell him."

"Okay." I followed my dad. I wanted to be there to support my grandfather, but I didn't know what to say to him. What do you say to a man who has lost his wife after so many years?

I watched as my dad crouched down and spoke to him. A moment later I saw my grandfather's head drop. I was suddenly feeling really bad for him. I thought about what it would be like to lose Guennie after a lifetime of memories.

My dad helped him out of the car and motioned for me to assist Grandpa over to the ambulance. I put my arm around his waist and supported him. His legs were weak and he was leaning on me. I helped him over to where Grandma was lying. Uncle Buddy and Aunt Gloria were on either side of her.

When they saw us, they both slid out. My grandfather sat on the gate of the ambulance and reached in to touch Grandma. He was saying something but I couldn't understand him. Then I realized he was speaking to her in Italian. I put my arm across his shoulders. It seemed like the right thing to do at the time. With his free hand, my grandfather grabbed mine and squeezed. I returned a tight grip. We stayed like that for five or so minutes.

Then he looked at me and smiled.

"She's with the angels now, Paulie."

I nodded and hugged him. He lifted himself from the back of the ambulance and looked at the fire, which by this time was just about out.

"We'll be okay," he said as he held the back of my head. "We'll be okay."

Chapter 20

A lot had happened in the last few days. My dad and his siblings arranged a memorial service for my grandmother. Instead of having a wake, they had a funeral Mass at St. Blaise in town and then invited guests to share a memory about her at the luncheon that followed the burial. It was all very nice. I learned a lot about her. The entire time the ceremony was taking place, I kept thinking about Guennie and how little time I had left with her. My dad promised I'd get a chance to say goodbye to her. I just wanted to make sure it was in private. I didn't want him listening in on our conversation.

I managed to have one last heart-to-heart conversation with Uncle Buddy about school. It took place the morning we left, on the back-porch swing, and it was life-changing.

"I have to be honest with you. Uncle Buddy, I'm basically just a C- student. And that's the best I'll ever be."

"If you want to be a C- student," he said, "then that's what you'll be."

"But I don't want to be."

He smiled. "Then what are you doing about it? Paulie, the future is in your hands. You can hide behind saying you're just a mediocre student all you want, but you can change that if you have the desire to."

"I do."

Uncle Buddy stood up and walked to the other end of the porch. "You know what? I think you're sabotaging yourself."

"Huh?"

"I think you're doing poorly in school on purpose to keep from qualifying for college admission. In your mind, not being able to get into a college is somehow better than flunking out of one."

I thought about what he had said. I didn't think I was consciously doing that, but it sure made a lot of sense.

"I guess I'm just afraid of—"

He walked back over and sat down. "'Always do what you are afraid to do.'"

"Is that an Uncle Buddy-ism, or another quote from Emerson?"

"Who else? It's Emerson," he said. "It's from his 1841 essay on heroism. Paulie, I can't tell you how many students I've come across at my school who are just like you—afraid of the unknowns at college."

As I listened, I realized he was absolutely right. Between Uncle Buddy and Guennie encouraging me to continue my education, I decided I wasn't about to disappoint either one. I made a personal pledge right then to study like never before, no matter what anybody else thought. I would apply myself, and then I'd find out once and for all if I really was a C- student. In my heart, I knew I wasn't. I knew I could get better grades.

And, boy, would I surprise some people—my dad, for one. I would get into a college if it was the last thing I ever did. I decided to give journalism a real shot. I would join the student newspaper, and I would ignore the critics who thought all student reporters were nerds. I would pay closer attention to the ten o'clock newscasts, and I would read the *Chicago Tribune* religiously. My dad would bring it home each day, set it on the coffee table, and I would usually ignore it. Not anymore.

Oh, and I promised Uncle Buddy his secret was safe with me.

The bar turned out to be a total loss, but the firemen had been able to save the house. Since Grandpa didn't have any business insurance, there was no money in the budget to rebuild the bar. My dad, Uncle Buddy, and Aunt Gloria went round and round about what to do with Grandpa. With his business gone, he couldn't support himself any longer. One of his children would have to welcome Grandpa into their home.

It didn't take my dad long to offer to bring his father to Chicago. He felt guilty about not being around for the past twenty years, and he wanted to make up for it. Grandpa would be able to live in our guest room. My dad did have to call my mom and discuss things with her. She put up little to no resistance.

Uncle Buddy would continue to teach, and to live in his mobile home with his partner, Jonathan. Mum's the word. And Aunt Gloria would have workmen tear down the bar portion of the structure, and she would reside in my grandparents' house rent-free. Her waitress job would help her pay the monthly bills.

My dad promised we would stop at the home of the sheriff's sister so I could see Guennie one last time and say goodbye as we left town. But first we would go to the cemetery to visit Uncle Dominick's grave. We had the option of doing so when we buried Grandma, but my dad said he couldn't handle both on the same day. When it was time to leave, everyone came out to the parking lot to wish us well.

"I can't believe you're leaving," Uncle Buddy said. "It's all gone too fast."

"I know," I said. "It flew by."

"I have high hopes for you, Paulie. You can go far. I know you can. And remember, whenever you need a little pep talk, I'm just a phone call away. Call me every once in a while, will you?"

"Absolutely."

He wrapped his arms around me and squeezed. I was going to miss him. He was the master motivator. I hoped I'd be able to call him on a regular basis from now on. I would need to hear his voice every so often. Uncle Buddy hugged my dad, who appeared somewhat lukewarm to the embrace. I finally knew what that was all about, but I didn't care. Uncle Buddy was a great guy. Period.

Then Uncle Buddy hugged Grandpa. They both started to cry. It made me tear up. There was something about seeing a man cry that always got to me. Aunt Gloria was less sentimental. She actually shook our hands rather than hugging us. Oh, well.

We hopped into the car. Grandpa insisted on sitting in the back seat. He let me ride shotgun. We drove about ten minutes through some pretty hilly terrain before we pulled up to the gates of the St. Michael Cemetery, the same place where we had buried Grandma. It appeared the place might be closed. My dad hit the horn a couple of times. About fifteen seconds later, a man appeared. He smiled, waved, and opened the gates. We drove slowly on a narrow dirt path. When we came to a fork in the road, my dad stopped the car.

"I'm trying to remember which way to turn," he said. "It's been a long time." He turned to his father. "Pop, do you know which way we go?"

"I'm sorry," he said. "I don't remember."

My dad eyed the surroundings for a minute and then turned left. "I hope this is right."

"Actually, it's left," I said, trying to be funny.

My dad made a face and kept driving. I should have known humor and cemeteries didn't mix. A moment later, the car slowed down to a crawl.

"It's somewhere over there," he said. "I think we can walk from here." He stopped the car and we got out. "I remember he was buried at the base of a big tree." My dad began walking, with me in tow.

I followed him up one row and down another.

We did this multiple times before he stopped and scratched his head. "I know he's here somewhere." He sounded frustrated. After ten more minutes of looking, he stopped short.

I nearly plowed into him.

"Let's split up." He pointed to his left. "You look in that area, and I'll go over there."

We parted. All of this walking was beginning to wear on Grandpa. He waited for us in the car. As I walked past endless graves, I found myself paying more attention to the inscriptions on each tombstone rather than looking for Uncle Dominick's gravesite. I noticed a lot of the headstones were chipped and faded. Some were leaning and others had been knocked over. The grass around them hadn't been cut in weeks. It was so high in places you couldn't even read the bottom half of the tombstone. I glanced over at my dad. He was standing with his hands on his hips. I could tell he wasn't happy. Since he had said Uncle Dominick was buried near a tree, I started looking at those graves exclusively. A few minutes later, when I had covered nearly three-quarters of the cemetery, I was starting to believe he just wasn't here. My dad must have made a mistake. I went back to where I had started my search and found him sitting on a headstone and shaking his head. He was quiet. I could tell it was best not to disturb him.

At that moment, I was more determined than ever to find the grave. I wanted to be the one who located it. I decided to re-inspect any of the graves within twenty feet of a tree. I began my hunt in a meticulous fashion. *No. Not here. Not this one. Or this one.* And on and on.

Then I spotted a tombstone that had fallen over. It was on the opposite side of a large oak tree. I must have missed it the first time around. I got down on my knees and tried to lift it. It was really heavy. When I had managed to raise it to about a forty-five-degree angle, I poked my head underneath and suddenly realized I had hit pay dirt.

This was it. I had found it, but I wasn't strong enough to flip it over.

"Dad!" I yelled. "I found it!"

He came running over. My grandfather joined us.

"This is it," I said. "But I can't lift it."

My dad got down, and the two of us together were able to prop it up. You could see now why it had fallen over. A huge tree root had grown directly under it and caused it to topple. It was hard to say how long it had been that way.

My dad straightened up in order to read the inscription:

HE DIED THAT WE MIGHT LIVE
U.S. ARMY PFC DOMINICK MARIO PASSERO
MARCH 10, 1921—DECEMBER 19, 1944

My dad's eyes began to water. He tried to hold back tears, but it was no use. He began to sob openly.

This was the first time I had ever seen my dad cry this way. I wasn't sure what to do. His head dropped. I knew I needed to do something, but I wasn't sure what. Should I say something? Should I do something? I waited several seconds and then I slowly extended my arm and put it around my dad's shoulders. The more he cried, the tighter I held him. My eyes were now watering. I didn't like seeing him cry.

"He was the best, Paulie." He fought to get the words out. "He was always there for me, but I wasn't there for him when he needed me."

I didn't say a word. I just let him talk. His breathing was labored. He raised his head and wiped his eyes.

"We can't leave him like this," he said. "He deserves better."

We slowly lowered the stone to the ground. I followed my dad to the car. We drove back to my grandparents' home in complete silence. We went into the garage and found a shovel. Then we drove back to the cemetery and dug a hole next to the tree root. We slid the stone into the new hole and placed dirt around it. When we were certain it was secure, my dad stood up, put his arm around me, and smiled.

From that day on, things were different between me and my dad. Oh, we still got into an occasional beef, but not nearly as often as we had before. After that, he rarely got on my case for anything bad that happened at school or at home. He never ragged me about them. He would instead try to find something positive to motivate me. He wanted me to learn from my mistakes.

I never told him, but I really appreciated the new approach. Allowing me to see him at one of his most vulnerable moments while at Uncle Dominick's gravesite seemed to have changed things between us. And it was so much for the better.

After we had finished setting Uncle Dom's gravestone in place, we got back into the car, and my dad pulled out a piece of paper. It read: "Anne Samuelson, 434 W. Pine Street, Leroy, PA." He put the car in gear, and we were soon on our way to the house where Guennie was now staying. He never once complained about having to stop there.

On the way, my grandfather made some small talk—things about missing his garden and his friends but looking forward to a new chapter in his life. It was mostly upbeat. He was a real trooper.

A few minutes later, we turned onto Pine Street. My dad slowed down the car and looked for numbers on the mailboxes. We stopped in front of a small home that seemed well maintained. No peeling paint. And the shrubbery was well manicured. It was very welcoming.

"Do you want me to go with you, or are you okay on your own?" my dad said.

"I'm good," I said as I stepped out of the car. I was suddenly nervous. I hadn't seen Guennie in a few days. I was hoping she still felt the same way about me as she had before. I climbed the stairs.

"I'm going to go gas up," my dad yelled from the

car. "I'll be back in a little bit. Take your time." He was really being great about this. He seemed to understand it would be better if Guennie and I had a little privacy.

I knocked on the front door. A few seconds later, a girl I had never seen before came out. She smiled at me. Then she stuck her head back inside.

"Guennie, he's here." She turned back to me and held out her hand. "I'm Corinne, by the way."

"Hi," I said. "It's nice to meet you. I'm Paulie."

Corinne put her hand over her mouth to keep from giggling. I wasn't sure what that was about. It was just something girls did, I guessed. I moved back a couple of steps and stared at the ground. Somehow I felt like I was being watched, but I didn't care.

"Hi, Paulie." It was Guennie. She stepped out from behind the screen door and joined me on the front porch. She looked absolutely gorgeous. Her eye wasn't red anymore, and it was completely open. The welt on the side of her face had faded. Her lower lip was no longer puffy. And for the first time, she was wearing a dress—a blue polka-dot sundress. She grabbed the edges of it and twirled around.

"Do you like it?"

"I love it."

"It's Corinne's. She let me borrow it. She's been really great about everything."

I smiled. "I am so glad you're in a nice, safe place."

"Me too. And you know what? Corinne's mom has been talking to the people at the county. She's trying to get approved as a foster mom so she can keep me indefinitely. Isn't that great?"

"It really is," I said. "I'm so happy for you."

"And there's more good news."

"What?"

"I'm headed back to school. I can't wait. I know most kids aren't very excited about going back to school in the fall. But I am, and I intend on making the most of it. I plan to study my butt off. I'm going to get into college. You wait and see."

I shook my head. "I have no doubt. I have a feeling whatever you set your mind to, you're gonna accomplish."

She motioned for us to sit down on the front steps. "So much has happened in the last couple of weeks," she said. "I almost can't believe it. And it's all because of you."

"I'm not so sure about that."

"I am. You saved me, Paulie. For the first time in my life, I feel like I've got a chance—a real chance to make it."

"You're gonna make it big," I said. "You're gonna get into a great college, graduate with honors, and have a successful career. You'll probably meet a nice guy, get married, and have a slew of kids."

She blushed. "Slow down, will ya, I'm still in high school."

We laughed. Then there was this awkward moment when neither of us knew what to say. We were both thinking the same thing—am I ever going to see this person again? We weren't sure how to say goodbye.

"So," she said. "Do you think you'll be making any more trips back to Leroy in the near future?"

"Absolutely," I said. But I was just dreaming. I had no idea when we might return. What were the chances my dad would want to come back to Leroy? To visit

Aunt Gloria? Ah, no. To visit Uncle Buddy? It was doubtful. They weren't very close. And now that Grandpa was coming to Chicago to live with us, there was no real reason for my dad to want to come back here.

Well, then, maybe I could come alone? Yeah, right. What were the chances my dad would let me take the car and drive six hundred miles by myself? It was impossible. Maybe I could rent a car? Yeah. Well, not really. I didn't have enough money for gas, let alone a car rental. And it was doubtful a sixteen-year-old kid could actually rent a car.

I was starting to believe this was the last time I would ever see her. If that were the case, then I wanted it to last forever. I wanted Guennie to be my girlfriend. I wanted to be with her for the rest of my life. But I knew in my heart it could never happen. My life was in Chicago. Hers was in Leroy.

Guennie pointed down the road. "Is that your car?"

I spotted my dad about fifty yards down the road. At least he had given us some space. There wasn't much time left.

"I just want to say…" I was having a hard time putting my thoughts into words.

"What?"

"I just want to say…these have been the two greatest weeks of my life. I'm really glad I got to know you. And I'm so glad you're safe now."

She put her finger under my chin and turned my face to hers. "Paulie Passero, I don't know if we'll ever see each other again, but I will never forget you. Never." She leaned forward and kissed me. Then, for what was probably the last time, I put my arms around

227

her, and held the kiss for as long as I could before I felt her pull away.

"Well, I'd better go," she said. She got up and walked over to the door. "Good luck and safe travels."

I didn't know what to say or what to do. I decided to let my heart do the talking. I walked over and hugged her. She kissed me on the cheek before she turned and reached for the door handle. I turned away, then turned back and waved. No words were coming out, so I ran down the steps and headed to the car.

When I looked back, she was still standing on the porch. I waved again. She waved back and disappeared behind the front door. I walked over to the car, got in, and closed my eyes. I wanted to cry, but I couldn't let my dad or Grandpa see me.

I put my head back, clenched my teeth, fought back the tears, and we were off.

Chapter 21

There was little to no conversation the entire length of the trip. I answered my dad's questions with one-word responses. I was a bit more cordial when Grandpa questioned me about things. I actually spoke to him in full sentences. For the ten-plus-hour trip, I had a chance to get to know him better. He was a nice old man who was being uprooted from the only home he had known for decades. I hoped he would be happy living with us. I would try my best to make that happen.

When my dad asked me to relieve him after we had crossed over the border into Ohio, I was glad. It would hopefully take my mind off Guennie. I put on a good face and continued to hide my disappointment. As much as I tried to think about other things as I drove, my mind kept bringing up images of her—in her cutoff jeans, in the post office, in the water at the swimming hole, in her house, in the front seat of our car, in the hospital, in Corinne's sundress. Every so often I would snap out of it. Then I would wonder how I had managed to drive with Guennie on my mind rather than concentrating on the road. It was a little scary, but somehow I had done it.

The entire time, I found myself trying to figure out a way to get back to Leroy. I wondered if there was a train from Chicago to Altoona, the closest train stop. I'd bet there was. But then what would I do for transportation once I got there? Was there a bus that stopped at Leroy? The entire time we had been there, I had never once seen a bus of any kind. A cab, maybe? No, that would be way too expensive. Wait a minute. Of course, Uncle Buddy. I was sure he would pick me up, and even let me stay at his place. That was how I would do it.

When I got home, I would check the train schedule. I wondered how much a train ticket cost. The next question was—when could I pull this off? School was starting in a few days. There was no way to fit in a trip before that. Maybe Christmas vacation was a possibility. Yeah, we would usually get up to two weeks off school. Now I had a plan. That was it. Christmas vacation it was.

Thinking about going back to Leroy took some of the sting out of saying goodbye. But how would she feel about me four months from now? A lot could happen in four months. She could meet someone and forget about me in no time. After all, she was now back at school—with boys galore. What were the chances no one would ask her out between now and Christmas?

The chances were slim. Since she would undoubtedly be the best-looking girl in class, how could the boys keep their eyes off her? Four months was a lifetime. Even if I did manage to buy a train ticket, and even if Uncle Buddy did offer to pick me up and let me stay with him, how would Guennie feel about seeing me again? She very possibly would have moved on with her life, and then how would I feel? Lousy, that was how.

I decided the only way to know if I should even consider trying to visit her would be to monitor the situation. I could do that through the mail. I would write letters to her. I had the address she was staying at, but I didn't have the post office box number for the sheriff's sister. I bet if I put the street address on the envelope, Norman at the post office would see it got to the right place. Sure, that would work. Then if she wrote back to me, I'd be able to judge by the tone of her letter if she was still interested in me or if she was just being polite. As soon as I got home, I would sit down and write to her. I didn't want to seem overly aggressive, but I just wanted her to know long distance relationships were possible; at least I thought they were.

When we pulled up in front of our house, I couldn't believe how quickly the time had flown by. My mom was waiting for us on the front porch. She had big hugs for me and my dad. She saved her biggest hug for Grandpa. He started to tear up. And then it was the full waterworks when Mom showed him his new room. She had spent a lot of time making it just right for him. I was hoping it would all work out.

"So how did you spend your time there, Paulie?" she asked.

I glanced at my dad, who shared a smile. "Oh, I kept myself busy."

"You should tell your mother the story about that girl," he said. "Your son was a hero."

"What are you talking about?" she said. "I want to hear all about it."

We sat down in the living room, and I told her the whole story. Not the mushy parts, of course. My mom sat on the end of the couch, speechless. She had never heard me talk about girls before. I think that part surprised her.

231

"You saved that girl's life, Paulie," she said. "Who knows how long that would have continued. You *are* a hero."

"I don't know about that," I said.

"Well, I do." She got up and hugged me. "You are an amazing young man." She kissed me on the forehead. "Mickey called earlier. I told him you'd be home soon. He said he might stop over later."

"Okay."

I went upstairs to my room and started to unpack. Then, for some reason, I felt really sad. I started to cry. I couldn't let anybody see me this way. I closed my bedroom door. And I locked it. I lay down on my bed, pushed my head into my pillow, and started bawling.

What was wrong with me? I had felt so great when I was with Guennie. Was it really over? Would I ever see her again? As much as I wanted to believe I'd return to Leroy someday, I doubted it. Would I ever have a relationship with another girl that would even slightly compare to what I had with Guennie? Right at that moment, it didn't seem possible. With my eyes closed, I just felt sorry for myself. I wasn't proud.

Maybe tomorrow would be a better day. I needed to get out of this funk. What could I do? And then it hit me—I could start on my letter to her. That might make me feel better. More connected.

I sat down at my desk, pulled a piece of paper from the drawer, and wiped the tears away.

Dear Guennie:

How are you? How are you making out with the Samuelson family? I hope things are going well for you. I think about everything that happened in the last two weeks and I can hardly believe it. I am so glad you have a new home with people who care about you.

When do you start school? We start next Tuesday, the day after Labor Day. In the past, with school less than a week away, I would start to get depressed, but I feel differently this time. I want to see if I can do better in my classes than before. And, honestly, it wouldn't take much for that to happen. I haven't been what you would call an academic scholar. I'm interested in seeing what grades I can get if I really apply myself.

I think I'm going to go over to the newspaper office at school and look into joining the staff. After watching what happened at the Democratic National Convention, I wondered what it might be like to be a newspaper reporter covering a story like that. I hope my writing is good enough for them.

How about you? Do you plan to get involved with any organizations at school? I'll bet you'd be good at whatever you tried.

Well, that's about it.

Paulie

P.S. I might try to visit over Christmas break. Looking forward to seeing you again.

I set down my pen and read the letter. It was okay, I guess. But it didn't sound like it came from someone who considered himself to be her boyfriend. I'd left out the part about how much I missed her. And I was crazy about her. And I loved her.

I had never felt this way about a girl before, so I wasn't sure how being in love was supposed to feel. Was it supposed to hurt this much? Was it supposed to rip out your insides? Was it supposed to make you weepy all the time? If this was how it felt to be in love, then I wasn't sure I wanted anything to do with it. But then when I remembered the times we kissed, and how it made me feel, then I couldn't get enough of it.

I heard someone coming up the stairs. I folded the letter and quickly stuffed it into my desk drawer. Then there was a knock at my bedroom door, but not just any knock. It was our secret knock. Three knocks followed by a scraping sound. Then three more knocks.

It had to be Mickey, or our secret was out. I wasn't sure if I was up to seeing him. It was nearly nine thirty, and after our ten-hour drive, I was exhausted. I wasn't really in the mood for idle chitchat, but I couldn't turn him away. He was my best friend. I walked over, unlocked the door, and opened it.

A smiling Mick stood in the doorway. "Man, you're back. I was going crazy with nothing to do while you were gone."

"I'm back, for what it's worth."

He sat down on my bed. "So how was small town USA?"

"It was fine," I answered matter-of-factly.

"Glad to be back?" he said.

"Yeah, kind of." I just sat there. I knew I wasn't my typical self, but I couldn't help it. There was a hole in my heart.

Mickey folded his arms. "Paulie, what's up?"

"What do you mean?"

"I know you, and I can tell when something's wrong."

I stared at the floor. "What are you talking about? Nothing's wrong."

He stood up, walked to where I was sitting, and hovered over me. "I'm not leaving here until you tell me everything."

I looked up and sighed. "You're probably not going to believe it, but it's all true."

He sat back down on the bed. "Let's go. Dish it."

For the next twenty or so minutes, I retold the story I had related earlier to my mom. But this time, I included the mushy parts. I could see his jaw drop a few times.

Mickey fell back onto the bed. "Paulie, that's a wild story. You should send it to *Detective Magazine*. They have some great *fiction* in there."

Just what I thought. He didn't believe me.

"Mickey, you can ask my dad about most of it. He can tell you it really happened."

"Even the kissing parts?"

"Well, he probably doesn't know about that."

"Just as I expected," he said. "Did you think all this up on the drive home today?"

I just shook my head. If he didn't believe me, there was nothing I could do about it.

"The last time I saw you," he said, "you were telling me how you were gonna make a play for Violet this year. Is that still on?"

"I just said that to get you off my back."

"Aha, I knew it. Well, don't worry, partner, if it's the last thing I do this school year, I'm gonna get you a date."

"I don't need your help."

"Well, you need somebody's help, that's for sure."

I decided to drop the whole Guennie story. There was no point in rehashing it. I would never be able to make Mickey believe me. And you know, I really didn't care. It happened. It was great. And maybe we'd get together over Christmas break. It was possible.

The thought of seeing her again kept me going. The next day I got a stamp from my mom and I mailed the letter. I hoped when Norman came across it, at the Leroy post office, he would make sure it got to her. He knew who she was, so I was fairly sure she'd get it.

The following week it was back to school. It was time for me to shine, if that was even possible. Junior year meant a heavy load: History, English, Math, Chemistry, and Spanish. I stuck to my guns and forced myself to study. I asked for fewer hours at the store. If I was going to turn things around, I would need more time to do it. For the first couple of weeks, I felt as if I was improving, but with a 78% on my first chemistry exam, I wasn't so sure. This was when I could have really used a pep talk from Uncle Buddy. But then I got nine out of ten on the next quiz, and I was pumped. Maybe I really could do this.

I did eventually wander into the newspaper office—the *Anton J. Cermak Gazette*. I asked them if I could get involved. They said they'd start me off with a fluff piece, just to see if I could actually write a real news story. Can you believe it? I was covering the Mother's Club Turkey Raffle. It was a little embarrassing, but I decided to make it the best Turkey Raffle story the *Gazette* had ever run. When my dad would bring home the *Chicago Tribune*, I would now pounce on it. I would read as many of the stories as I could. I wanted to write a story the same way the *Trib* reporters did.

When I handed in my Turkey Raffle story, I gave it to Tom Harrison, one of the senior editors. I watched Tom as he read it, word for word. When he had finished, he looked up, smiled, and shook my hand.

"Welcome to the *Gazette*, Paulie." My next assignment was to write a profile piece on a teacher who was new to Cermak that year. Not an earth-shattering assignment, mind you, but definitely a step up from the Turkey Raffle. I attacked it with the same vigor as I had done the first time.

Nearly a month had passed, and I still had not heard from Guennie. I fought the urge to send a second letter before she had responded. I knew it would make me look desperate. I wondered why she had ignored my letter. Maybe she'd never received it. Maybe she had moved on with her life and wanted to put the past, including me, behind her. Maybe she was too busy with friends and classes and such.

I thought back to the last day I had seen her, when she told me she would never forget me. Was she just saying that because it sounded good? Or did she mean it? You would think, if she meant it, she could spend fifteen measly minutes writing a letter. I began to feel the two weeks in Leroy had meant a lot more to me than they had to her.

And lo and behold, after I had given up all hope, there was a letter waiting for me on the living room coffee table the next afternoon when I got home from school. The return address said *Guinevere Thompson*. I could feel my heart beating right through my chest. I took several deep breaths.

This was it. This is what I had been waiting for. My future with Guennie would be made known once I opened this envelope and read the contents of the letter. I was hoping—praying even—she would say some of the mushy stuff we never had said to one another but we actually felt, or at least I did. I imagined myself tearing open the envelope and hearing Guennie say she would wait for me no matter how long it took—that there was no one else like me—that we were destined to be together.

I took the letter and ran upstairs to my room. I needed to be alone for this. I was worried it would be really bad and I might start crying again. I couldn't let anyone see me. It was embarrassing enough the first time. I had to learn how to fight back the tears, to suck it up, and to be a man. I tore open the envelope and read the letter.

Dear Paulie,

I got your letter a few weeks back. Thank you. I'm really sorry it's taken me so long to write back. I don't have any excuses. I just kept putting it off. Please forgive me.

Well, a lot has happened since you left. Maybe your uncle told you about it. My dad was being held in the Leroy jail. About a week ago, they decided to move him to the county jail. While the transfer was taking place, my dad overpowered one of the county guards and wrestled his gun away from him. He shot the guard in the shoulder. The second county guard and Sheriff Middleton fired back. My dad was hit three times in the chest. He died right there. There was no funeral or memorial service. They buried him in an unmarked grave in a cemetery on the outskirts of town.

Please don't judge me, but I haven't visited the grave yet. I'm not sure if I ever will. Now he can't hurt me anymore, and that is a huge relief. I hope you understand.

And that brings me to the topic of my brothers. As hard as he tried, the sheriff couldn't pin the fire at your grandfather's bar on my brothers. I'm sure they did it. It's exactly the type of thing they would do. Well, they apparently got bored with farm chores and tried to hold up a liquor store in town a few days ago. The problem was the owner of the store had a gun. He held them there until the sheriff arrived.

When the Van Dyke County District Attorney talked to them, he painted a very bleak picture of their futures. My two older brothers took a plea. They'll serve a minimum of eight years and no more than twelve.

My youngest brother was sent to a juvenile detention facility. A day later, he escaped. And no one has seen him since. I know it sounds cruel, but I hope I never see any of them again.

Corrinne and her sister and her mom have been great to me. Mrs. Samuelson treats me just like another one of her own daughters. It's really nice. I'm finally a member of a real family, not like before. The sheriff told me since my dad didn't have a will, the county will probably auction off our farm. The money will then be split four ways. I didn't know how I'd be able to pay for college. Now I have a way.

Oh, one last thing. I've met a lot of kids at school. Some I already knew. There's this new boy named Brad who kept trying to talk to me. I wasn't interested at first. I thought he was weird. But the more I got to know him, the more I realized he wasn't weird at all. He was normal, and he's really nice. There's a homecoming dance at school next month, and Brad asked me to go. Don't be mad, but I said yes. I was pretty sure you'd understand. I'm sure you'll be asking some girl at your school to your homecoming.

Well, gotta go. I hope things are okay on your end. Until next time.

Guennie

Until next time? Until next time? That's how she signed off her letter? Would *Love, Guennie* have killed her? And who the hell was this Brad guy? He was probably a real jerk. I'd like to take him apart. It was pretty convenient for him to make time with my girl while I was away. Who did he think he was anyway? Wouldn't he be surprised if I suddenly showed up in Leroy. I'd bet he's not counting on anything like that. I crumpled up the letter and threw it across the room. I sat down on the bed and fell back onto my pillow. She was the first girl I ever loved. How could she do this to me? She *thought* I'd understand? Well, let me tell you something, Guennie—I *don't* understand. How would she like it if I found somebody else? I doubted if she'd understand.

The more I thought about it, the more I realized my two weeks with Guennie was just that—two weeks with Guennie. We had some fun. We had some tender moments. And we had some drama. But it ended right there. When she kissed me goodbye on that porch, it was goodbye forever. How could I have been so naïve as to think we would ever become an item? We were two ships passing in the night—nothing more.

I walked over to my desk, sat down, and opened my chemistry book. I had to read the chapter on deoxyribonucleic acid. I got out my highlighter and got to work, or so I thought. I tried to read. I really did.

But it was no use. I kept thinking about her. I skipped dinner that night and went to bed early. I told my mom I wasn't feeling well. And depending on how you look at it, I guess that wasn't really a lie.

When I woke up the next morning, I thought I'd be over her. Instead, I didn't want to get up. I didn't want to face the world. I finally managed to drag myself out of bed, into the bathroom, down the stairs, and up to the breakfast table. I did my best to make small talk with my parents, but my heart just wasn't in it.

When I got on the Belmont bus, I waited for Violet to get on. I figured a good dose of Violet, heavy black eyeliner and all, was what I needed to help me forget Guennie. But when the bus stopped at her corner, a few members of her posse hopped on, but no Violet. It figured. The day I needed a little something to pick up my spirits had turned out to be a repeat of the day before, when I was at my lowest point.

Mickey was sitting next to me on the bus, making some inane chatter about something or other. I didn't even hear him. I was deeply entrenched in my own self-pity, with no plans to climb out.

When we got to school, I fumbled for a few minutes at my locker and then took off for Mr. Drennan's English class. I would have a real difficulty concentrating today. We had to discuss Aldous Huxley. I'll tell you one thing—Mr. Drennan had better be on his game. He needed to keep me both awake and interested.

As was the routine, I ducked and dodged other classmates in the hallway on my way to first period. But then, only steps away from class, I spotted her standing by her locker—Andie—Andrea Walker. I could suddenly feel butterflies in my stomach. Before there ever was a Guennie, there was Andie.

She looked great today. She had her hair pulled

back in a high ponytail. It was the way she usually wore it on the tennis court. There was no one around her. I would never have a better chance to talk to her one on one. But then I remembered I could never work up the nerve to talk to girls. I would just stand there like an idiot. I'd open my mouth and babble. What was the use? I kept walking. I was getting closer and closer to her. I looked away.

And then something hit me. I had just spent the last couple of weeks with a girl, a really beautiful girl. We talked. We laughed. We hugged. We kissed. If I could talk to Guennie, I should be able to talk to Andie. Right? Or would the same thing happen? Would I freeze? Talking to Andie would certainly take my mind off Guennie. But could I do it? Did I have the guts to walk right up to her and start a conversation?

I was no more than ten feet away from her. *It's now or never, Paulie. Just do it, man.* I drifted over in her direction and took a chance. Was I ready to have my heart broken twice in one twenty-four-hour period? I was about to find out.

"Hi, Andie," I said.

She turned and smiled. "Oh, hi…Paulie, is it?"

"Yeah."

"You sit at our lunch table, right?"

"That's me," I said.

She closed her locker. "You're pretty quiet during lunch."

"I guess I'm just too busy chowing down."

She laughed.

"You know, I meant to tell you—I'm a really big fan of yours. You know, on the tennis court. I've seen a bunch of your matches. Against Madison, Greendale,

Roosevelt. Against a bunch of schools."

"I don't ever remember seeing you in the stands."

"Oh, I was there. I guess I just blended in with the bleachers." Actually I was hiding behind the bleachers.

"Well, thanks for your support," she said.

"You know, someday I'd love to learn that sport," I said.

"Maybe I can show you sometime," she said.

We started together down the hall. I walked right past Mr. Drennan's classroom. I wasn't going to blow this chance.

"Now that would be great. I would love that."

An awkward pause followed. And then she totally knocked me out.

"What are you doing this Saturday?" she asked. "We have practice from ten till noon. Why don't I meet you on the tennis courts at twelve?"

"Perfect. I'm embarrassed to say I don't even have a racket."

"That's no problem. I have plenty." She glanced at the clock overhead. "Ooh, I'm gonna be late. So I'll see you on Saturday...at noon."

"It's a date," I said. "I'll see you then."

"Well, bye." And she was gone.

Oh, my God! What had just happened? Was I going on a semi-date with Andie Walker? This was amazing. I couldn't believe it. And she was the one who suggested the time and place. She could have easily blown me off. But she didn't. And you know what? I had just talked to a girl. I had actually done it. And I hadn't babbled. I actually kind of made sense. I ran into Mr. Drennan's classroom and plopped into the desk right in front of Mickey. I was beaming.

I turned to face him. "Guess who has kind of a date with Andie Walker on Saturday?"

"What are you talking about?" he said.

"I told you. I'm meeting Andie this weekend."

Mickey folded his arms. "Is this another one of your stories?"

I thought about it for a moment. "Yeah, kind of."

"More fiction, huh? Get outa here. You don't have to make up stories about girls. I told you—I'll get you a date, Paulie. Just give me some time."

I sat back in my seat. "Take all the time you need, Mick." In the background, I could hear Mr. Drennan's voice. But I had no idea what he was saying. I was too busy basking in the glory.

I thought about Guennie's letter. I'd been pretty sore when I read it. But I was starting to feel better about it now. I had finally come to the realization that I would probably never see her again—that we lived in separate worlds—that we needed to follow our own paths.

But I would never forget her. She had taught me a great lesson—how to talk to girls—how to act around girls—how to show your affection for girls. She'd made it easy for me to talk to Andie.

I never could have done that without Guennie. I needed to thank her for that.

Thanks, Guennie. Thanks for everything.

So it looks like the Summer of Guinevere has become the Autumn of Andie.

A word about the author...

John Madormo, Chicago-area screenwriter, author, and college professor, has created a body of work that has attracted the attention of motion picture producers and publishers. John sold a family comedy screenplay to a Los Angeles production company, signed a contract for a three-book deal with a major New York publisher, and was named the Grand Prize winner of a national writing competition.

He has five books published elsewhere for young readers, featuring a 12-year-old private detective who sets up shop in his parents' garage and solves cases for fellow sixth-grade classmates. The books have been embraced by educators on a national scale, including various Battle of the Books programs, and one of the books was nominated for the 2015-16 Iowa Children's Choice Awards. Another was added to the kids' recommendation list of the International Spy Museum (Washington D.C.). Scholastic's Book Experts gave five-star reviews to all the books in the series.

John also has a middle-grade series titled The Adventures of Rutherford, Canine Comic being published elsewhere, with Book 1 to debut in winter of 2019.

John has placed in numerous screenwriting competitions, including as Grand Prize winner in the Reno Film Festival Best Synopsis Contest, and took First Place for Best Family Film Synopsis.

In addition, he has entered into option agreements with several motion picture production companies.

Find out more at http://www.johnmadormo.com or http://www.summerofguinevere.com

Thank you for purchasing
this publication of The Wild Rose Press, Inc.

For questions or more information
contact us at
info@thewildrosepress.com.

The Wild Rose Press, Inc.
www.thewildrosepress.com

To visit with authors of
The Wild Rose Press, Inc.
join our yahoo loop at
http://groups.yahoo.com/group/thewildrosepress/